All About Marilyn

Also by Shawn James

ISIS

THE CASSANDRA COOKBOOK

If you have questions and comments about this book send your E-mails to Shawn James at:

sjsdirectny@aol.com

And check out Shawn James' blog at:

shawnsjames.blogspot.com

All About Marilyn

A Screenplay by Shawn James

That page with the legal stuff on it

Copyright © 2008, 2009 Shawn James. All Rights Reserved.

All About Marilyn ISBN: 978-0-615-34258-0

WGA Registration Number # 1285126
Library of Congress Catalog number # PAu 3–361–159

Published by SJS DIRECT, 1294 Grant Avenue Bronx, NY 10456. No part of this book may be reproduced or transmitted in any form or by any means, graphic, electronic, or mechanical, including photocopying, recording, taping or by any information storage or retrieval system, without permission in writing from the publisher and Shawn James.

Front cover art "Abstract Sista" designed by and © Shawn James

Printed in the United States of America

This is a work of fiction. All events, locations, institutions, themes, persons, characters and plot are completely fictional. Any resemblance to places or persons, living or deceased, are purely coincidental.

Dedicated to all the black actresses whose performances in television and black cinema inspired me to create many strong black female characters in my writing. You'll always be superstars in my eyes.

Acknowledgments

I would like to thank God for helping me write this book. If not for Him, I would have never finished this story. With His help maybe I'll be able to take my craft to the next level.

I'd also like to thank my Mother for supporting me and my writing career all these years.

A special thanks to my brother Steve for inspiring me and giving me hope during some of the hardest times of my life.

I'd also like to thank my sister Shawna for giving me a copy of Syd Field's *Screenplay*. That book helped me learn the basics about screenwriting and helped me learn a whole new set of writing skills.

I'd also like to thank all those wonderful African-American book clubs who took the time to read and review *The Cassandra Cookbook*. I'm hoping everyone continues to support my writing career with this book.

In addition, I'd like to thank fellow writers Liz Issacs and Francine Craft who commented on my blog and gave me advice that helped me further develop my writing craft.

Finally, I'd like to thank my POD printer. If not for this great technology, this screenplay would be sitting at the bottom of a closet forgotten for years to come.

Screenplay Basics

If you've never read a screenplay before, don't worry. I'm going to walk you through some of the terminology used in a movie script.

FADE IN: – The opening line of every screenplay. It tells the reader what they're looking at in the opening scene.

INT. – Short for Interior. This heading is used to describe action in scenes going on indoors.

EXT. – Short for Exterior. This heading is used to describe action in scenes going on outdoors.

Both of these headings usually start at the top of a SLUG LINE.

SLUG LINE – The sentence at the beginning of a scene that tells the reader where the scene is and what time it's happening. Some examples of slug lines are:

INT. MARILYN'S APT – MORNING

This scene is inside Marilyn's apartment and it's in the morning. However, if she goes into another room in the apartment like the–

KITCHEN

A shorter slug line can be used since the action is still taking place inside the apartment. And if she decides to step outside later–

EXT. 14th STREET – NIGHT

A new slug line will tell the reader the action is taking place on 14th Street at night.

Screenplay Basics

MAJOR CHARACTER names like MARILYN MARIE are written in ALL CAPITALS when they are first introduced and in dialogue headings. Basic English grammar applies for all story paragraphs and the descriptions of minor characters like extras. An example of this is:

Sitting quietly between an early 20s CLOWN and a late teens mime is MARILYN MARIE, 34.

The Clown and Marilyn are major characters; the mime is a minor character.

INSERT – The camera moves from the main action to a shot of something relevant to the story. Usually inserts are pictures of objects like clocks or action going on a TV screen or computer monitor.

CUT TO: – The camera moves away from the main story to another shot rapidly then back to the main action.

POV – Used to show us what goes on in the eyes of the character. We see what the character is seeing.

BACK TO – Used to transition from an insert or a cut back to the main action.

MOVING – This is usually used to describe action in cars, planes and other vehicles.

BRRRING! The phone RINGS. KA–BOOM! The bomb EXPLODES. CRUNCH! He takes a fist to the jaw! SOUND EFFECTS are always CAPITALIZED.

PARENTHESES (Wrylies) – These are simple stage directions placed under a section of dialogue for the actor. These are used only when absolutely necessary. Actors hate it when there are too many wrylies in a script. It's not the writer's job to tell actors how to act!

Screenplay Basics

VOICE OVER (V.O.) – Usually placed under a section of dialogue to describe when someone is speaking off screen. In this screenplay I'll be using the term (ON PHONE) to describe most of the voice-overs.

MONTAGE – A series of quick scenes that move the story forward. Usually montages are set to music onscreen. They often show time passing or transition from one story sequence to another.

DISSOLVE TO: – Used when one scene fades into another. Dissolves are another way of transitioning between two scenes to move the story forward, but like wrylies dissolves are used when absolutely necessary. It's the director's choice where these are placed in the final film, not the writer.

No matter how the story is written, all screenplays end with:

FADE OUT:

THE END

All About Marilyn

FADE IN:

INT. APEX STUDIOS STAGE 22 – AFTERNOON 1996

An upscale Beverly Hills mansion set decorated with high-end 1990's living room furniture and Christmas decorations. Actors go into character when the DIRECTOR yells...

                  DIRECTOR
        ACTION!

The action on set cuts to–

INSERT

Videotaped action on a monitor. Two poor GIRLS, 7, and 9, are presenting a Christmas gift to NIKKI DESMOND, 17, a spoiled rich brat wearing trendy mid 1990's designer clothes. Her butler RUMSFELD, 65, a polished British servant stands at her side as they address her.

                  GIRL #1
    Miss Nikki, we'd like to thank you for all your
    volunteer work at the community center.

                  GIRL #2
    Yeah, we got you a gift. All us kids chipped in
    to buy it.

Nikki rolls her eyes and requests–

                  NIKKI
    Rumsfeld, could you get that for me?

Rumsfeld takes the box from the anxious kids and walks over to Nikki. Anticipation builds as–

She opens the box. Not happy with her gift. She rolls her eyes and asks–

                NIKKI
What the hell is Mainframe?

                GIRL #2
It's a t-shirt like all the girls in our class wear.

                GIRL #1
Yeah, we got it from Sears.

Nikki scoffs and tosses the shirt on the floor like it was diseased. Rumsfeld picks it up gingerly.

                NIKKI
SEARS? YOU BOUGHT ME A SEARS SHIRT!

                GIRL #1
Y-You don't like it?

Nikki turns to Rumsfeld to ask him–

                NIKKI
Rumsfeld, what would I use this for?

                RUMSFELD
Why Miss Desmond, you'd use this to wax the Rolls.

The girls are disappointed on cue when the Director yells–

                DIRECTOR
...And cut. Print it. It's perfect.

On the call of cut the action moves from the monitor –

BACK TO STAGE 22

Where the actors break out of character. Nikki Desmond is actually MARILYN MARIE, 22, a sweet sista with girl next-door features.

All About Marilyn

Rumsfeld is TREVOR BARTLETT, 63, an old black English theater veteran. The girls are HANNAH CYRUS, 8, and TABATHA STRONG, 10, seasoned white child actors. All eagerly wait for instructions from the Director who tells them—

> DIRECTOR
> Okay everybody, that's a wrap. Take lunch. Be back here by three.

The production crew hustles around the set as Marilyn turns to the kids with a kind smile. Her voice deepens to a sultry adult tone as she tells the girls—

> MARILYN
> You guys did great! I'm so proud of you!

> TABATHA
> Thank you Miss Nikki.

> MARILYN
> Er— Tabatha, my name is Marilyn in real life.

> TABATHA
> Sorry Miss Marilyn.

> MARILYN
> It's okay.

> TABATHA
> When I grow up I wanna be a star just like you.

Marilyn smiles as the girls run off to the arms of their parents. Trevor turns to Marilyn to ask her—

> TREVOR
> Marilyn, will you be joining Christopher and me for lunch?

MARILYN
I'd love to Trev, but I've got that lunch with the Apex Studio reps.

TREVOR
The developmental deal for the feature films? Oh, I do hope it works out for you.

MARILYN
I'm crossing my fingers. Lucy and everyone at Burbank Baptist is praying for me.

The concerned Director overhears the conversation. He looks at his shooting schedule and inquires–

DIRECTOR
You're going to be back here to shoot the haunting scene at four right?

MARILYN
I'll probably be here before then. I'm only going to be across the lot.

DIRECTOR
Great. I'll have wardrobe bring the nightgown to your dressing room at three.

MARILYN
Oh, can I borrow Garrett for an hour? It's kind of important.

The Director smiles. He's eager to please his star.

DIRECTOR
Sure. I'll get the script supervisor to collate the pink pages.

Marilyn rushes off the set down a–

All About Marilyn

HALLWAY

Bustling with action. Stage Hands and Set Decorators carry props and bedroom furniture to the set. They smile at Marilyn as they pass her by. She turns into the–

DIRECTOR'S OFFICE

A crazy cluttered office space. Anxiously waiting at the copier spitting out pink pages is GARRETT WILLIAMS, 22, a young black ambitious production assistant. He lights up when Marilyn walks into the room and gives her a pound.

                    GARRETT
Mari Mari. What's up?

                    MARILYN
A lot. You have your screenplay?

Garrett fishes through a pile of crumpled script pages on his desk and comes up with his completed screenplay.

                    GARRETT
Right here.

                    MARILYN
Great. I told Sabrina to meet us over there.

The script supervisor walks in as they hurry off the set to–

INT. APEX STUDIOS EXECUTIVE OFFICES RECEPTION AREA – AFTERNOON

An executive waiting area decorated with high-end office furniture and fresh cut flowers. Marilyn and Garrett are awe-struck. They meet up with–

SABRINA LOWENSTEIN, 55, a savvy agent who knows her way around Hollywood like the back of her hand. She hugs Marilyn tightly and smiles at her. Garrett feels the love as they break the embrace.

> SABRINA
> How are you Marilyn?

> MARILYN
> Nervous Bri.

> SABRINA
> Don't worry. These sharks don't bite.

The trio heads past the receptionist into–

HIRAM SILVERSTIEN'S OFFICE

A luxurious office suite with a great view from picture windows. At his desk is HIRAM SILVERSTIEN, 56, a Hollywood power player dressed in a tailored black Italian business suit and red power tie. On the phone is MARTIN ROSENTHAL, 45, a slick studio lawyer. Martin hangs up the phone and both men give Marilyn a once-over as they get up. They like what they see.

> MARTIN
> Ms. Lowenstein, Ms. Marie, this is Hiram Silverstien, director of developmental properties.

Hiram shakes everyone's hands then gestures to a sofa and chairs across the room. Sabrina, Marilyn, and Garrett sit on the sofa; Hiram and Martin in the chairs. They're ready to get down to business.

> HIRAM
> From what I see Ms. Marie, you have a lot of potential. Your show's ratings are in the top ten with teen and tween boys and girls and your Q rating is through the roof. I think

All About Marilyn

you're ready to branch out into projects for a broader audience.

The trio gets anxious— it's happening!

MARILYN
What type of projects are you considering me for?

HIRAM
I want to do three films with you so I can get a feel of how the audience responds to you. From there we'll see about expanding your brand outside of the All About Nikki show.

Sabrina gives Marilyn an eager look. She wants this to work out for her. Marilyn is excited.

SABRINA
If things work out this could be your big break.

MARILYN
I could be on my way.

HIRAM
I'm hoping so.

MARILYN
I think I've found the script that's perfect for me.

Marilyn jumps up off the sofa and grabs Garrett. Hiram and Martin scowl at him.

MARILYN
Gentlemen, this is Garrett Williams, the writer of SELL OUT.

Garrett extends his hand and the executives give him weak handshakes. He hands Hiram his screenplay. Hiram nonchalantly flips through it and passes it to Martin—

> HIRAM
> Marilyn, this is an interesting idea but it's not the direction I want to take you in.

A befuddled Marilyn presses on—

> MARILYN
> I feel you should give this script a chance. It's the kind of material that will allow me to show audiences I can play something other than Nikki Desmond—

> HIRAM
> I understand your passion for this script Ms. Marie, but a project like this could do severe damage to your brand.

> MARILYN
> But it's a great script—

> HIRAM
> But not for you. You appeal to teens and tweens. Their parents would be shocked if they saw you in something urban like this.

Marilyn understands the racial undertones of what Hiram is saying. Martin peers up from the pages of Garrett's script to ask—

> MARTIN
> Did you read the script our readers sent to you?

> MARILYN
> (Scoffing)
> Dark Ride? I needed a shower after reading it.

All About Marilyn

HIRAM
I feel it's perfect for you. It'll allow audiences to see you as more sophisticated, edgy–

MARILYN
It's Nikki Desmond in a haunted house.

HIRAM
It's a horror-thriller-comedy like SCREAM. Big right now.

MARILYN
There was a lot of profanity in there–

MARTIN
It was a rough draft. It's being rewritten as we speak.

HIRAM
Would you be comfortable doing sex scenes and nudity–

Marilyn gets nervous.

MARILYN
I don't know about this–

HIRAM
It's only partial nudity. Like the stuff they do on NYPD Blue. Nothing too risqué–

MARILYN
You don't have another script for me to look at–

Sabrina sees a deal falling apart. She steps in–

SABRINA
Gentlemen, can we have a minute?

Marilyn and Garrett follow Sabrina out to the–

RECEPTION AREA

Where Marilyn expresses her concerns.

          MARILYN
Bri, this doesn't feel right–

          SABRINA
I know. But an opportunity like this isn't going to come around again–

          MARILYN
I just don't know about this. Nude scenes, profanity, it just isn't me–

          SABRINA
Honey, it's just a character–

          MARILYN
I just want to make sure it doesn't reflect badly on mine.

          SABRINA
If you show everyone who you are on the inside they'll love you with or without clothes on.

          MARILYN
I still wish I could do Garrett's movie–

Garrett supports his friend the only way he can.

          GARRETT
Look Mari, this is your big break. You can't pass this up. Not for me, not for nobody. You got to take this.

All About Marilyn

MARILYN
You sure about this?

GARRETT
Hell yeah. If it's meant to break for me it'll break for me. You just do your thing.

Marilyn reluctantly agrees with her friends. She looks Garrett directly in the eyes as she promises–

MARILYN
I'm going to do everything in my power to make sure SELL OUT gets made.

Garrett smiles as they walk back into–

HIRAM'S OFFICE

Martin and Hiram smile when Sabrina announces–

SABRINA
So when do we start shooting?

HIRAM
We're casting right now and scouting locations, so shooting should start right around the end of the season.

SABRINA
Great. That gives Marilyn time to prepare for the role. What are you offering in terms of compensation for this developmental deal?

MARTIN
We're prepared to offer Ms. Marie our standard contract regarding percentages on residuals of box office, syndication, and home video. Salary wise Apex Studios will offer one million dollars up front.

Sabrina bristles at the offer. She knows Marilyn is worth twice as much.

> SABRINA
> For each picture?

> MARTIN
> For all three pictures.

> SABRINA
> That's really low—

> HIRAM
> We believe we're offering fair compensation to an untested property—

> SABRINA
> Fair for who?

Marilyn sees a deal falling apart. She steps in—

> MARILYN
> Bri, it's okay. I accept your offer.

> SABRINA
> Marilyn, are you sure about this?

> MARILYN
> Yeah, Bri. I guess all we have to do is shake hands and the deal is done.

Hiram smiles as Marilyn and Sabrina seal the deal with handshakes. Martin peers up from Garrett's script to close the meeting—

> MARTIN
> I'll have those contracts delivered by the end of the week Ms. Lowenstein.

All About Marilyn

> SABRINA
> Thank you gentlemen.

Martin is eager to get back to Garrett's script. The group leaves the office and heads down the–

OFFICE HALLWAY

Where Sabrina expresses her concerns.

> SABRINA
> Marilyn, I think you should have let me try to get you more–

> MARILYN
> I don't think we were going to get a better offer Bri–

> SABRINA
> Yeah, but after I take my ten percent, your manager takes his fifteen percent, you pay your publicist, pay your taxes, and give your tithes to Burbank Baptist there isn't going to be much for you to live off of–

> MARILYN
> I'll be okay. I'm just sorry I couldn't help Garrett get his big break.

> GARRETT
> It's cool Mari. Thanks for having my back in there.

> MARILYN
> I never left your side.

> GARRETT
> I mean it was just great being here. Meeting the executives, pitching my script–

                SABRINA
It usually takes fifteen years to get this far—

It hits Garrett in the head about his screenplay.

                GARRETT
Oh man! I left my screenplay in there!

                SABRINA
Don't worry about it. Is it registered with the WGA?

                GARRETT
And the Copyright office.

                SABRINA
Don't sweat it then. Worse comes to worse they throw it away—

                GARRETT
Or they could read it. Maybe SELL OUT could be your second film Mari.

                MARILYN
Maybe...

DISSOLVE TO:

MONTAGE

Movie reviews in newspapers. All bad. Headlines read:

a) "Dull Ride is All About Boring."
b) "This ride is the end of the road for Nikki Desmond."
c) A September 1997 Variety article detailing how Dark Ride flopped at the box office opening in 23rd place.
d) A November 1997 headline in the TV section of the Los Angeles Daily News stating: "All About Nikki series to end in May."

All About Marilyn

e) Marilyn holding a letter dated June 3, 1998 stating Marilyn Marie is released from her Apex Studios developmental contract.

The yellowed page turns twelve years later in—

INT. 1989 MERCEDES 500SL CONVERTIBLE – MORNING PRESENT DAY

MOVING

The passenger seat of an old faded red Mercedes convertible driving past Burbank's big movie and TV studios. The letter in a paper protector falls inside the distressed leather binder of an OLDER MARILYN MARIE, 34, a beautiful black woman dressed in a once trendy poet blouse and worn out once-popular designer blue jeans. Still the sweet girl next door at heart. She looks past her headshot down at the schedule page then down the block at—

EXT. DOWNTOWN BURBANK – MORNING

A bad part of town. Rundown buildings from another era. Marilyn parks her car on the street and walks up to a—

RUNDOWN OFFICE BUILDING

And BZZT! Hits the intercom button. She's greeted by a hostile female—

              VOICE
  Who is it?

             MARILYN
  I'm Marilyn Marie from AATA. I'm here for
  the reading—

BZZT! The buzzer abruptly opens the grimy steel security door. Marilyn walks into—

INT. RUNDOWN HALLWAY – MORNING

A seedy smoke-filled walk up. She heads upstairs to–

G-TOWN PRODUCTIONS

A low-budget production company. The posters of previous productions taped to the walls are direct-to-video crap like bad action movies, exploitative "hood" movies, and soft-core porn. Marilyn walks up to the receptionists' desk– she's busy on a personal call. She gestures to the back room where Marilyn finds–

BACK OFFICE

A tight space. Outdated video equipment, old office furniture, and stacks of DVDs share space with staff. Sitting behind the desk is JOEY JACKSON, 28, a wanna-be Hollywood big shot dressed in a cheap suit and tacky jewelry. Across from him at the editing table is Director RON JENKINS, 25, in hip-hop gear. He has less talent than Joe and less class. Lounging on the sofa is KWON, 19, in hip-hop gear. Just here to look at the hotties. He recognizes Marilyn–

>KWON
>OH SHIT! IT'S NIKKI DESMOND!

An embarrassed Marilyn smiles politely as the G-Town crew get a good look at her. She feels their eyes crawling all over her body as Joey introduces his staff.

>JOEY
>Marilyn, I'm Joey Jackson, president and CEO of G-Town, that's Ron our director, and chillin on the sofa is m'man Kwon our talent scout.

Marilyn shakes hands and gives out headshots. Joe drops his on the desk covered with pictures of a who's who of once popular black actresses from over the past decade. Marilyn anxiously waits for instructions from–

All About Marilyn

JOEY
You're reading for Linda right?

MARILYN
Yeah.

Marilyn prepares to go into character. Ron has second thoughts.

RON
Joe, I ain't feeling her as no Linda.

Marilyn is about to walk away. Joe gestures for her to stop.

JOEY
Look man, we need a name on the case to sell the DVD to retailers–

RON
I hear you Joe, but I'm not feeling her.

JOEY
Ron, she's perfect for the part. She got a cute face and a nice smile–

RON
Cute? Man, get out of here with that shit. Homegirl got to be what? Thirty, thirty-two at least with them crow's feet around her eyes. Ain't nobody gonna believe her old ass can pass for twenty-one.

JOEY
Ron, good black don't crack. And this sista ain't porcelain. I got a good feeling about her.

RON
Look, if we cast her all people gonna do is point to screen and scream Nikki Desmond. Nobody gonna see our story.

                    KWON
Yo, don't let that smile fool you man. Any o'yall remember that episode where she made that old lady cry? That shit scares the shit out of me to this day.

An embarrassed Marilyn scowls at Kwon who pretends to cringe. Ron uses it to his advantage.

                    RON
See? People buying our movie ain't gonna believe her as no nice girl you take home to momma. One look at her and all they gonna see is that ol' ball busting bitch from the TV show.

                    KWON
I hear you Ron. She'll make people break their suspension of disbelief.

                    JOEY
Man, who else we gonna get to play lead for $1500? I don't see no Halle Berry or no Jada Pinkett busting down the door to be in our movie—

                    RON
Joe, we spend money on her we gonna lose it at retail. $1500 is gonna cost us $350,000. I'm just sayin'.

Money takes Joe off the fence. Marilyn tries to change his mind.

                    MARILYN
Look, I'm not like that at all. Just let me read for it—

Joe isn't budging.

All About Marilyn

                JOEY
I'm sorry, but I can't have Nikki Desmond in my movie.

Marilyn keeps it professional.

              MARILYN
Thank you for your time.

Before the dejected Marilyn walks out Kwon requests–

              KWON
Yo Nikki, can a brotha get a autograph?

Marilyn takes Kwon's headshot signs it then shuffles out the office downstairs to–

EXT. DOWNTOWN BURBANK STREET – MORNING

Where she's about to get in her car. BRRRING! Her cell phone rings. Marilyn answers it–

              MARILYN
Marilyn Marie.

              SABRINA
             (On phone)
Marilyn, this is Sabrina. I need you to come down to the agency right away.

              MARILYN
I'll be there in a couple of minutes.

Marilyn gets in her car and drives down to–

EXT. DOWNTOWN BURBANK OFFICE TOWER – MORNING

A better part of town. Marilyn parks, walks into the–

INT. LOBBY – MORNING

and passes by a–

NEWSSTAND

Plastered with magazine covers and tabloids featuring stories about an ADULT TABATHA STRONG, 22, America's white blonde superstar. Marilyn frowns and rides the elevator up to the–

14th FLOOR

A Berber carpeted workspace. She pushes past glass doors to enter the–

ALL-AMERICAN TALENT AGENCY RECEPTION AREA

A D agency, a place people go for their first acting jobs. Framed posters of past hit shows and headshots of top clients hang on the walls. A frazzled RECEPTIONIST, 23, peers up from the stacks of files on her desk with fresh headshots jutting out as–

Marilyn walks in. She hits the intercom button and tells her–

              RECEPTIONIST
I'll let Sabrina know you're here.

              MARILYN
  Great.

Marilyn has a seat on the crowded leather sofa between an early 20s CLOWN and a late teens mime chatting on a cell phone. She anxiously clutches her cracked leather portfolio, sighs, and looks across the room at the–

All About Marilyn

ALL ABOUT NIKKI POSTER

Depicting her at 17 in similar early 1990's designer clothes. Benetton, Gap, Generra. A rich spoiled brat sitting on the hood of a shiny red 1989 Mercedes 500SL convertible with a smug smile on her face. The supporting cast standing behind her on the mansion steps looks annoyed. The Clown notices the poster then inquires–

> CLOWN
> Hey, aren't you Nikki Desmond?

Marilyn is embarrassed about being recognized.

> MARILYN
> Yeah, I used to play her.

> CLOWN
> Man, I used to love that show when I was a kid! I loved how you used to tell people off and shit–

> MARILYN
> I'm glad you enjoyed the performance.

> CLOWN
> Man, I wish I could be like you. I'd tell my boss where he could stick this clown suit.

Marilyn is uncomfortable. She wants to change the subject.

> MARILYN
> So… you're a clown?

> CLOWN
> It's just something I'm doing until I get my big break. Y'know Nikki, in a couple of years I want to be just like you. Nice car, big mansion–

MARILYN
Marilyn. My name is Marilyn.

CLOWN
I thought you were Nikki–

MARILYN
Nikki Desmond was the character I played. My name is Marilyn. Marilyn Marie.

The Clown looks befuddled.

CLOWN
I–I'm sorry er– Marilyn. I guess I got caught up in the character.

MARILYN
It happens.

CLOWN
So what are you here for? Pick up a big royalty check? Inside track on a movie–

MARILYN
A call. Just like you.

CLOWN
I guess your agent swore you to secrecy about this project? What is it? Drama? Comedy? Reality show? I bet it's something to give Paris Hilton a run for her money–

MARILYN
I'll find out when she tells me.

CLOWN
Are the clothes for the role too? What is that? Vintage Gap? All you need is the Blossom hat–

All About Marilyn

Marilyn is about to answer when the receptionist hangs up the phone.

                RECEPTIONIST
    Ms. Marie, Sabrina will see you.

Marilyn is relieved.

                MARILYN
    Thanks.

Marilyn hurries past reception, down a corridor turns a corner and pauses at the—

ASSISTANT'S DESK

Stacked high with files. On the phone is Sabrina's young hungry assistant AVA GARDNER, 28, wearing a designer gray business suit. She eyes Marilyn like fresh meat as she walks into the open door of—

SABRINA'S OFFICE

An executive's home away from home. Staring out of picture windows at Downtown Burbank is an OLDER SABRINA LOWENSTEIN, 67, a crusty silver haired beauty in a crisp gray business suit. She sees Marilyn and her dull eyes light up.

                MARILYN
    So what's up Bri?

                SABRINA
    Close the door Marilyn. Have a seat.

Marilyn closes the door. Outside—

                                    CUT TO:

Ava hangs up phone and rushes over to the door. Inside—

SABRINA'S OFFICE

Marilyn and Sabrina take seats in the leather chairs in front of her glass-topped desk. Sabrina somberly looks at the pictures of Marilyn next to ones of her kids before telling her–

SABRINA
I'm retiring.

Marilyn is shocked.

MARILYN
I–I don't know what to say–

SABRINA
Nothing to say honey. I've been in this business for forty years. I'm tired of it.

MARILYN
It can take a lot out of you working all these long hours–

SABRINA
(Laughing)
You're so sweet Marilyn. That's why I'm telling you this face-to-face.

MARILYN
I take it everyone else is getting a form letter.

SABRINA
Everyone else will have another agent by the end of the week. At least you care about me.

MARILYN
So this call isn't about a gig?

All About Marilyn

SABRINA
No. I wanted to give you some advice before I left. Get out of this business. Get out before it kills you.

Marilyn is shocked about the request.

MARILYN
You want me to retire? I'm 34—

SABRINA
That's exactly why you need to get out. You have your whole life ahead of you.

MARILYN
Bri, I'm still getting work—

SABRINA
Come on Marilyn, the only auditions I send you on nowadays are guest spots on cable shows, crap parts in B-movies, or you work some bullshit comic convention signing autographs. You don't want to spend the next twenty years dealing with that shit.

MARILYN
Bri, all I need is one good role to make people forget about Nikki—

SABRINA
Marilyn, you can't keep doing this to yourself—

MARILYN
I have to work—

SABRINA
What are you working for?

MARILYN
I don't know. I just want to get past Nikki Desmond—

SABRINA
Honey, Nikki's living the high life in syndication and you're losing the best years of your life trying to get away from her ghost.

MARILYN
This is just a slump—

SABRINA
Slump? It's been ten years since you last worked steady. You're in freefall.

MARILYN
Bri, it's not that bad. I still have my royalties—

SABRINA
Honey, I've seen those checks. They're so small I don't even take my ten percent. All About Nikki royalties won't even get you a Whopper and fries at Burger King.

Marilyn concedes to Sabrina's truths.

MARILYN
That's before taxes.

SABRINA
I've seen a lot of good kids like you lose everything because they were too scared to move on.

MARILYN
Is that what you're afraid of? Me winding up on drugs or a mental case—

All About Marilyn

SABRINA
Something worse. I'm afraid you won't let the acting bug go.

MARILYN
What do you mean?

SABRINA
Kids like you hold onto acting because it's all you know and you're afraid to try something else. You know the boat is sinking, but you're so scared of drowning you go down with the ship.

MARILYN
Either way I'm in the water.

SABRINA
I don't want to help you drown.

MARILYN
That why you're retiring?

SABRINA
It's my job to look out for your career. I'm hoping this will get you swimming to land before it's too late.

MARILYN
If I'm not acting, what do you suggest I do to make a living?

SABRINA
Go out and have some fun.

MARILYN
That's not an answer–

SABRINA
It's not meant to be. Just give yourself a shot out there.

Both women get up. Sabrina hugs Marilyn tightly. Marilyn breaks the embrace and knows Sabrina loves her like family.

MARILYN
I'll think about it.

A worried Marilyn opens the door as–

Ava bolts back to her desk. She pretends she's on the phone, then follows behind Marilyn as she leaves the AATA office. She swoops in like a vulture when Marilyn pauses at the–

ELEVATOR BANK

AVA
(Extending hand)
Ms. Marie?

MARILYN
Yes?

AVA
Ava Gardner. I couldn't help but overhear your conversation with Sabrina–

MARILYN
(Shaking Ava's hand)
I'm no longer her client.

AVA
Well, I'd like to offer you my services of representation–

MARILYN
You're an assistant.

All About Marilyn

> AVA
> Agent-in-Training. I'm building a list of clients and I'd love to have a valuable AATA property like you on my list.

Marilyn realizes what's going on.

> MARILYN
> Sabrina's body isn't even cold yet and you're harvesting organs.

> AVA
> I can get you a supporting part in a movie–

> MARILYN
> Yeah right–

Marilyn doesn't want to hear it. She reaches for the elevator button. Ava grabs her arm–

> AVA
> Look, I've read the breakdowns. This part is perfect for you.

> MARILYN
> Please. You don't even have a SAG card–

Ava pulls a card out of her blazer.

> AVA
> Licensed and bonded by the state of California. One job is all I'm asking you to do with me. You don't like it, fire me.

Marilyn is tempted. Ava smiles. She has her hooked.

> MARILYN
> You have a script?

                    AVA
    I'll call you with the details this afternoon.

Ava presses the down button. Marilyn gets on the elevator and rides downstairs. She leaves the building and heads out to–

EXT. DOWNTOWN BURBANK STREET – MORNING

Where she gets in her convertible. She starts it up and drives downtown to–

BURBANK BAPTIST CHURCH

A big gothic looking building with colorful stained glass windows. Marilyn parks out front and enters–

INT. BURBANK BAPTIST CHURCH LOBBY – MORNING

A warm cozy place that feels like home. The full list of services on the board includes a soup kitchen, food pantry, and counseling. Marilyn heads downstairs and turns the corner into the–

CAFETERIA

A big empty lunchroom filled with empty tables and chairs. Church staff gets ready for dinner services except for–

REV. GREGORY WILLIAMS, 60. A good salt of the earth Christian dressed in a white polo shirt and khakis. He's sitting reading his newspaper when Marilyn approaches–

                  GREGORY
    Hey Marilyn, I didn't see you at breakfast.
    What happened?

                  MARILYN
    I had an audition Reverend.

All About Marilyn

GREGORY
Oh, how'd it go?

MARILYN
The usual.

The Reverend expresses his sympathies in the only way he can.

GREGORY
Don't worry, God will work things out. Just keep trying.

MARILYN
Thanks. Is Lucy around?

GREGORY
She's in the pantry doing inventory.

MARILYN
Thanks.

Marilyn walks out of the cafeteria, into the kitchen, and turns the corner into the–

PANTRY

With aisles of shelves stocked like a supermarket. Counting canned goods in solitude is LUCIA BARETTO, 34, a kind Mexican woman dressed in khakis and a white polo shirt. She smiles at Marilyn and asks–

LUCIA
Hey Mari, how'd your audition go?

MARILYN
I got roasted Lucy. Extra crispy.

LUCIA
Well, this should cheer you up.

Lucy hands Marilyn a shopping bag filled with groceries. She lights up at the sight of–

>MARILYN
>Kashi! Oh, thank you so much Lucy!

>LUCIA
>We should be thanking you. If you hadn't talked to the manager down at Ralphs last week we wouldn't have gotten this donation yesterday.

>MARILYN
>You want me to help you with inventory?

>LUCIA
>Nah, I'm done here. I was about to go back to my office and you were about to tell me about your problems.

>MARILYN
>I'm that transparent.

>LUCIA
>You haven't changed that much since high school.

The women laugh, walk down the hall up the stairs to–

LUCIA'S OFFICE

A nice cozy corner filled with old comfortable office furniture. The plaque on the door reads "LUCIA BARETTO EXECUTIVE DIRECTOR OF COMMUNITY PROGRAMS". Bachelor's and Master's degrees from Stanford University hang on her walls next to framed articles from newspapers detailing her church community work. An autographed picture of Marilyn sits on her desk next to teenaged pictures of them hanging out together. The women take seats and Lucy asks–

All About Marilyn

LUCIA
So how bad was this one Marilyn?

MARILYN
Bad. Sabrina is retiring Lucy.

Lucia gasps then regains her composure.

LUCIA
It's for the best. God knows what He's doing.

MARILYN
She says she did it for me to wake up.

LUCIA
The life of an actress is like a dream. No matter how bad the fantasy is, sometimes it's more painful to wake up and face reality.

MARILYN
She wants me to get out of the business.

LUCIA
Maybe it would be best.

MARILYN
What would I do? I've been acting since I was seventeen–

LUCIA
You could go to college–

Marilyn shakes her head. One of the big regrets of her life.

MARILYN
You know it's too late for that Lucy. I blew my shot at Stanford to be on TV–

LUCIA
Come on, you used to get all A's back when we were in high school. I think you could do it–

MARILYN
And how would I pay for it? I work for food around here–

LUCIA
Come on, God has always made a way for you Marilyn. He'll make a way for you to go to school if that's what you want.

MARILYN
Yeah, it has been a miracle I've been able to keep my bills paid these past five years.

LUCIA
See? You just have to trust God.

MARILYN
I guess you guys won't be getting that big donation from me anytime soon.

LUCIA
You do enough. Helping us cook in the kitchen, serving up meals, delivering groceries–

MARILYN
I was on my way to the gym. You want me to take some stuff over to the seniors?

LUCIA
No, you make it all about Marilyn for a while. Just remember, you don't have to be a star to be a light.

All About Marilyn

                        MARILYN
            I'll remember.

Marilyn leaves church, gets in her car, and drives cross-town. She parks in the lot of—

EXT. JIM'S GYM PARKING LOT – MORNING

A big modern building with lots of new top shelf luxury cars parked outside. Mercedes, Audi, Lexus, BMW, Jaguar. Marilyn's old Mercedes sticks out like a sore thumb.

Marilyn pulls a gym bag out of the trunk and walks into—

INT. JIM'S GYM LOBBY – MORNING

A high-end sports club. Hardbodies work out on machines and walk around. Marilyn reaches into her bag and swipes an ID card through the reader at reception then heads into the—

LADIES LOCKER ROOM

A luxurious changing area filled with teak benches, marble tiled floors, and Turkish towels. Hardbodies undressed. Marilyn drops her bag, opens her locker, and looks across the room. She smiles when she sees—

DR. SHAYLA SIMS, 34, across from her. A strong confident sista with a tight body, she's half dressed in powder blue sweatpants and a matching sport bra. She smiles back at Marilyn and gives her a pound.

                        SHAYLA
            Hey Marilyn.

                        MARILYN
            Hey Shay. I'll be ready in a minute.

Marilyn unbuttons her blouse as—

                              CUT TO:

Two pairs of Italian high heels pound across the tiled marble floor. She–

                              CUT TO:

Turns to be confronted by–

NATALIE JACOBS, 35, and HOLLY EVANS, 33. A pair of rich white blonde snobs wearing designer business suits. They lean on the locker doors between Marilyn and point daggers at her. Marilyn sighs and takes off her blouse.

                    NATALIE
          Hey look, it's the Movie Star.

Marilyn turns the other cheek.

                    MARILYN
          Is the gym crowded?

                    HOLLY
          No. Everyone else is at work. We have jobs to
          go to.

Marilyn hangs her blouse on the locker door. Natalie snatches it off the hook. Shay is concerned but Marilyn gives her a look. She's handling it.

                    NATALIE
          Oh, a poet blouse. I haven't seen one of these
          since college. My butler uses old rags like this
          to wax the–

                    MARILYN
               (Snatching blouse back)
          It was for an audition.

All About Marilyn

               HOLLY
Are you really an actress? Y'know I never see
your movies at the theatre or on cable–

Marilyn stuffs the blouse in her locker then takes off her sneakers and jeans. Natalie and Holly's claws come out seeing Marilyn's toned stomach and defined legs.

               NATALIE
No Holly, remember we found one of her
DVDs down at the supermarket. It was in the
99-cent bin.

               HOLLY
Yeah, we laughed our asses off watching it
Saturday Night. What a piece of shit–

               NATALIE
You did a great job handing change to the
customer in that store scene. Maybe you'll be
ready for the real thing in a couple of years.

Holly pats on Marilyn's stomach–

               HOLLY
Better lay off the abs Movie Star. You're
starting to look like a dude.

The withdrawn look on Marilyn's face makes their day. The women grab their Gucci bags–

               HOLLY
Come on Nat, we've got to go to work. We
can't be like the Movie Star here sitting
around working on our six-pack and our tan
all day.

Natalie and Holly sneer at Marilyn then leave. Marilyn ignores them, unzips her gym bag, and changes into a red spandex crop top and shorts. After she ties her hair into ponytail and wraps a towel around her shoulders, she and Shay hit the–

GYM FLOOR

Most machines are available. Marilyn and Shay walk across the room to series of treadmills in the front window. When they hit their stride Shay tells a brooding Marilyn–

> SHAYLA
> Nikki Desmond would have told both those bitches off.

> MARILYN
> I start acting like her and I'll never be myself.

> SHAYLA
> And the fantasy will become your reality. One of the two catch-22's of being typecast.

> MARILYN
> The other is being popular enough to be recognized, not popular enough to get work. I'd love to just get away from Nikki once and for all. Find a character that would make the world forget she exists.

> SHAYLA
> You still wouldn't be yourself.

> MARILYN
> I'd be working.

> SHAYLA
> You still wouldn't be yourself.

> MARILYN
> I'd be somebody to them.

All About Marilyn

SHAYLA
But you still wouldn't be yourself.

MARILYN
I can never be myself Shay. I play other people for a living.

SHAYLA
You're yourself with me.

MARILYN
You don't watch TV anymore.

SHAYLA
That's why I'm so well balanced. So how has real life been treating you Marilyn?

MARILYN
Kicking me in the tits as usual. I got roasted in yet another audition and now Sabrina is retiring.

SHAYLA
I'm sorry.

MARILYN
You know what's funny? I come out of the meeting and her assistant starts pitching to me. Says she's going to get me a part in a movie.

SHAYLA
Sounds like standard business in this town. Watch out.

MARILYN
I'll give her a shot. I want to do one last job.

SHAYLA
You're a little young to be talking retirement–

MARILYN
I just want to make enough money to pay for college. I always wanted to go when we were kids–

SHAYLA
Yeah, while Lucy and I were at Stanford studying, you were taping the show and shooting that movie. What was it called– Dark Ride?

Marilyn remembers the movie. Bad memories.

MARILYN
Not too many people remember that steaming pile. I think it was in the theatres about a week–

SHAYLA
I read the box. The plot sounded like something out of a MST3K feature–

MARILYN
Don't tell me you found it–

SHAYLA
I was buying fruit for Thomas and they had it on the dollar rack. I had to buy it.

MARILYN
So what did you think?

SHAYLA
You better go to college girl.

All About Marilyn

MARILYN
That bad.

SHAYLA
Why don't you come out to New York with me? You could stay with us–

MARILYN
You know Terrence wouldn't go for it. I can hear him ranting now: "I don't care how many TV shows the heifer been on she ain't stayin' in my house!"

Shayla laughs at the imitation. Marilyn is dead on.

SHAYLA
Come on, back in the day we used to invite you in our house every Monday night. This wouldn't be any different–

MARILYN
I left when you changed the channel.

SHAYLA
I don't want to leave you like this–

MARILYN
Hey, this is something I have to do for myself.

Both women at a fast pace. Heart rates up. Ready to move on.

MARILYN
Want me to spot you on the bench?

SHAYLA
Yeah. How long are we staying today?

MARILYN
Until two. We're going to do a circuit.

Shay slides off the treadmill and gives Marilyn a look.

> SHAYLA
> Am I going to be in one piece when I pick up Thomas from Day Care?

Marilyn hops off the treadmill and smiles.

> MARILYN
> I'm not going to work you too hard.

Both women head over to the weight machines. They work out on equipment until Marilyn checks her watch. 2:00. A sweaty Marilyn and Shay head off the floor into the–

LADIES LOCKER ROOM

Shayla opens her locker and gets undressed. Marilyn opens her locker and takes out flip-flops and store brand bodywash. She turns the bottle upside down–

And finds the sliver of soap inside won't get her past lather and rinse. She's contemplating options when–

Shay wrapped in a white towel grunts. Marilyn turns around–

To be presented with a new bar of Dove. She smiles.

> MARILYN
> Wow. Dove. I haven't bought this brand in years.

> SHAYLA
> Beats staring that trickle of soap down the bottle.

> MARILYN
> I'm going to pay you back.

All About Marilyn

                    SHAYLA
    Just get me out of here before three and we'll
    call it even.

Marilyn strips down and gets into flip-flops and a towel. They shower, get dressed, then head out to the—

EXT. PARKING LOT – AFTERNOON

Marilyn's watch reads 2:35 when they pause between her old convertible and Shayla's shiny new Mercedes SUV. Shayla dressed in jeans and a blouse reaches into her purse and pulls out three hundred dollar bills. Marilyn frowns at the money.

                    MARILYN
    Put your money away Shay.

                    SHAYLA
    Girl, take this money. I'd have to pay a trainer
    twice as much to get a body this *foine*.

                    MARILYN
    Are you sure?

                    SHAYLA
    I'd rather give it to you to spend on groceries
    than watch Terrence spend it on Playstation.

Marilyn reluctantly stuffs the money in her pocket. She really could use it.

                    SHAYLA
    I'll see you Friday.

Shayla gets into her SUV; Marilyn gets into her convertible. They both drive off in different directions—

EXT. MARILYN'S MERCEDES – AFTERNOON

MOVING

Marilyn drives down city streets then past a sign reading SERENITY TOWERS. She stops at a security terminal near the front gates and punches in a code. The gates open–

And she drives down a path towards a luxury hi-rise. Marilyn eases her car off the driveway into the–

SERENITY TOWERS PARKING LOT

A private lot filled with new top end luxury cars parked in rows. Bentley, Lexus, Audi, Mercedes, BMW. Marilyn parks in spot 3C and is approached by–

LORI LEWIS, 52, wearing a blue business suit and scrutinizing a clipboard. She has a button stating "TOWER BOARD PRESIDENT" on her lapel. The position makes her feel important. Marilyn gets out of her car and tries to keep the peace.

                MARILYN
What can I do for you Lori?

                LORI
Marilyn, I'd like to talk to you about your vehicle. The other tenants here feel it doesn't reflect the image of Serenity Towers.

                MARILYN
I can't afford a new car right now–

                LORI
We understand your financial situation. But we feel you could use some of the equity in your apartment–

All About Marilyn

MARILYN

Hold on. You want me to get back into debt because you feel my car doesn't fit in with the other cars around here?

LORI

It's part of the rules of occupancy here at Serenity Towers. Code 13. Section 8. Page seven. All tenants will keep well-maintained vehicles in the parking lot.

MARILYN

My car is well-maintained. I just took it to the mechanic–

Lori peers down at the odometer. Sneers. Writes a ticket.

LORI

Compared to other vehicles in the lot, this is not a well-maintained vehicle. There's 185,667 miles on the odometer, your paint is scratched, the finish is dull, your headlamps are yellowed–

MARILYN

You're going to write me up over a car I've driven in and out of here for over fifteen years? I don't believe this–

LORI

Look, it's not All About Nikki around here. You have to follow the rules like everyone else.

MARILYN

Look, you know I can't afford a new car right now–

                              LORI
If your financial situation prevents you from conforming to Serenity Towers community standards, then perhaps you should consider relocating. You have 45 days to buy another vehicle or we take you to the Board. Good day Ms. Marie.

Lori hands Marilyn the ticket and walks away. Marilyn points daggers at her, then takes a deep breath and gets her groceries and gym bag out of the trunk. The Doorman lets her in as she skulks into the—

INT. SERENITY TOWERS LOBBY – AFTERNOON

Decorated with marble floors, ferns, and fresh cut flowers. A fountain across from the concierge desk. Marilyn gets on the elevator and rides up to the—

THIRD FLOOR HALLWAY

Decorated with a painting on the wall, and paisley Berber carpets. Marilyn approaches Apartment #3C and opens the door of—

INT. MARILYN'S APARTMENT LIVING ROOM – AFTERNOON

A museum chronicling the career of a once-popular teen star. Framed posters of All About Nikki and Dark Ride hang in the foyer. Across from them are framed 1990's TV Guide, Ebony, Jet, Essence, People, US, YM, Right On!, Cosmopolitan and Seventeen magazine covers with her on them next to a page of a 1995 People article listing her as #36 of People's 50 most beautiful people. On the adjacent right wall are framed Neutrogena, Gap, and Cover Girl ads with her in them are followed by a collage of photos of a popular teen star hanging out with celebrities at 1990's trendy spots. An All About Nikki standee is in the corner next to a mahogany bookcase filled with videotapes. A crystal clear bowling ball prop and promotional items from the show are displayed on

All About Marilyn

the top shelf between a set of boxed All About Nikki dolls. Marilyn crumples up the ticket, throws it in the trash, takes a videotape out of the bookcase and walks into her–

BEDROOM

A neat master suite decorated with old top of the line mid 1990's furniture. The pictures on the dresser are stark contrast to ones in the living room. The intimate photos show a young woman with family, reading the Bible to kids in Sunday school, cooking in the church kitchen, helping Lucy and church staff with a bake sale, and posing in the gym with Shayla. Poor but happy. Marilyn drops her bags, smiles, and pops the tape in the VCR. She kicks off her shoes, flops onto the bed, and watches–

INSERT

An episode of All About Nikki on TV–

INT. DESMOND MANOR LIVING ROOM – MORNING

Nikki waits impatiently at the bottom of the stairs while her maid ROSA, 36, timidly shuffles downstairs carrying a red sweater.

                  ROSA
    Miss Desmond, your red cashmere sweater.

Nikki glares at sweater then snatches it from Rosa.

                  NIKKI
    This isn't my red sweater. This is my crimson
    sweater!

                  ROSA
    They look the same–

A pissed off Nikki tosses the sweater in Rosa's face.

NIKKI
Maybe they're the same in your country, but not here in America. Now go upstairs and get my red sweater.

Rosa skulks upstairs. Rumsfeld walks into the room followed by Nikki's FATHER, 45, a well-dressed businessman. He's angry about the way Nikki is behaving.

RUMSFELD
Miss Desmond, which one of the cars shall I bring around?

NIKKI
I really want to make the kids jealous. Let's take the Rolls to school today Rumsfeld.

FATHER
Rumsfeld, hold off on bringing the Rolls around. Nikki's not going anywhere until she apologizes to Rosa.

RUMSFELD
Very good sir.

Rumsfeld leaves the room. Nikki's Father lets into her.

FATHER
Nikki, you can't talk to people like that. Now go upstairs and apologize to Rosa.

NIKKI
Dad, Rosa's not people. She's help.

Nikki's outraged Father wants to take a belt to her. He holds back and says–

FATHER
She has feelings just like you do–

All About Marilyn

BACK TO MARILYN'S BEDROOM

Where she's getting into the episode as–

BRRRING! Her phone rings. Marilyn reaches over to the phone on the night table–

          MARILYN
Marilyn Marie.

          AVA
          (On phone)
Marilyn, this is Ava. I wanted to give you the details on the project. Meet me–

Marilyn has a bad feeling about this. She remembers Dark Ride.

          MARILYN
Meet you? What's this project about?

          AVA
          (On phone)
I'll give you the details when you come down to the set. It's shooting on location at 3800 Wilshire Boulevard tomorrow–

          MARILYN
Casting in the middle of shooting? I don't like where this is going–

          AVA
          (On phone)
I thought you wanted this job–

          MARILYN
This is short notice. If I'm reading for a supporting role you should be Fed Exing me a script right now–

                    AVA
                 (On phone)
Don't worry. This is a great project. It's going
to pay six figures.

                  MARILYN
        (Grabs a pad off the night table)
3800 Wilshire?

                    AVA
                 (On phone)
See you tomorrow morning at seven.

Marilyn hits end. She hops out of bed and grabs the box of Kashi cereal out of the bag. The old episode plays until the–

NEXT MORNING

A lone Kashi flake floats in a bowl of milk next to an open Bible on the night table. The TV broadcasts the morning news doing a live feature on–

INSERT

A cheery Tabatha Strong on location at Wilshire Boulevard. She smiles for the camera like America's sweetheart–

                  TABATHA
        Yeah, on location shoots are like, so cool. I
        get to like spend so much time with my fans
        in between takes. You never know what's
        going to happen–

As Tabatha blathers–

BACK TO MARILYN'S BEDROOM

Marilyn sprawled out on the bed in panties awakens–

All About Marilyn

And peers up at the clock. Six A.M. Her eyes grow wide noticing the time—

> MARILYN
> Oh man, I can't believe I overslept! I can't be late for this audition!

Marilyn springs out of bed and hurries into the—

BATHROOM

A clean and luxurious bath suite with marble counters, gold faucets, and a glass-enclosed tub. Marilyn washes her face, puts on lipstick, deodorant, and brushes her hair silky smooth. She then streaks—

BACK OUT TO THE BEDROOM

Where she rifles through a closet of once trendy old clothes. GAP, Tommy Hilfiger, Rampage, ESPRIT, Girbaud, Generra, Ralph Lauren, Benetton. Marilyn finds an old black and white floral rayon print slip dress that's passably stylish and puts it on. She steps into a pair of old black cowboy shoes, grabs her portfolio, and hurries downstairs out to the—

EXT. PARKING LOT – MORNING

Where she gets into her Mercedes and peels off. She doesn't have a moment to lose. The freeway traffic is going to be crazy.

The sun rises as Marilyn arrives at—

WILSHIRE BOULEVARD

Six-fifty-five, city streets are quiet. Marilyn sees production trucks, trailers, and staff several blocks down in front of skyscrapers. She finds a parking spot, gets out of the car with her portfolio, and walks down to—

3800 WILSHIRE BOULEVARD

A metal barricade up front, hundreds of people on the street. Security guards glare at Marilyn until–

Ava cuts through them wearing a production tag around her neck. No script in hand. Marilyn has a bad feeling about this.

                  AVA
She's with me.

The guards let Marilyn through the barricades.

                MARILYN
I'm not on the list?

                  AVA
Don't worry about that.

                MARILYN
Why shouldn't I? You don't have a script, I'm not on the list–

A Production Assistant heads over to Ava and Marilyn ready to get to work.

          PRODUCTION ASSISTANT
Ava, you need to get the extras staged around the commissary tables for attendance.

                  AVA
Will do.

PA walks away. Marilyn is pissed. She grabs Ava–

                MARILYN
Extra? You said this was a supporting role!

All About Marilyn

                    AVA
            (Pulling out of grip)
    Look, you do the extra work, network with
    the producers and you might be able to work
    it into a larger supporting role.

Marilyn glares at Ava who reassures—

                    AVA
    This is going to work out. Trust me.

Ava walks Marilyn over to the—

COMMISSARY TABLES

A big breakfast buffet. Extras and crew chow down and schmooze. Ava disappears into crowd, but a familiar face spots Marilyn—

And she spots him. An OLDER GARRETT WILLIAMS, 34. A fine intelligent brother dressed in jeans, sneakers, a button down shirt, and a SELL OUT ball cap. He holds a shooting script binder in his hands and has a production tag around his neck. They both give each other big hugs.

                    GARRETT
            (Breaking embrace)
    Mari. Man, I haven't seen you in years. How
    you doing girl?

                    MARILYN
    Surviving Garrett. You still a PA?

                    GARRETT
    Man, I've come a long way since then. I got
    my greenlight.

Marilyn is elated. Garrett hands her his screenplay. She flips through—

MARILYN
This is *your* movie?

GARRETT
Yep. We're shooting SELL OUT.

MARILYN
(Handing him his script back)
It looks like they didn't change it too much.

GARRETT
It's a miracle it made it through rewrites this much intact. But they are giving me a nice fat production budget.

MARILYN
How much?

GARRETT
$100 Million.

MARILYN
Wow. The studio must really be behind you–

GARRETT
We're on schedule for a July 4 release next year.

MARILYN
Are you still casting?

GARRETT
Man, we completed casting six months ago. The only scene with a lot of extras is this one.

Garrett's statement confirms Marilyn's suspicions.

MARILYN
Just like your old draft.

All About Marilyn

GARRETT
So what brings you by Mari?

Marilyn looks around. Ava is gone. She realizes she's been set up. She pastes on a smile–

MARILYN
(Extends hand)
Oh– I just came down to congratulate you. Good luck on your project Gar.

GARRETT
(Shaking hand)
Thanks Mari. I'll be looking out for you on my next project.

A PA grabs Garrett and walks him away. Marilyn hears Joey Jackson's voice in her head–

JOEY
(V.O.)
I'm sorry, but I can't have Nikki Desmond in my movie.

And realizes she shouldn't be here. She slinks into the crowd and passes by the Clown out of makeup. A skinny, clean-cut kid wearing jeans and a T-shirt. He brushes his friend–

CLOWN
Hey man, Nikki Desmond is here! HEY NIKKI!

Marilyn turns; the Clown's friend reaches into his pocket for a digital camera as they walk over to her.

MARILYN
I told you my name is Marilyn.

                    CLOWN
See man, I told you I met Nikki yesterday!

                CLOWN'S FRIEND
                (Raising camera up)
Can– can we get a picture?

An awe-struck look on his face. It's his first time seeing a real live star. Marilyn doesn't want to disappoint them.

                    MARILYN
One picture.

                    CLOWN
Cool.

Both men stand around Marilyn. Another one of the Clown's other friends positions the camera. FLASH! Picture with big smiles. The camera's flash alerts others in crowd. Young kids. Late teens early 20s. They grew up watching the show. They instantly recognize Marilyn–

                    FAN# 1
HEY THAT'S NIKKI DESMOND!

And rush up to her pulling out cell phones, digital cameras, sheets of paper, and pens–

                    FAN #2
OH MY GOD! IT IS NIKKI!

                    FAN #3
Oh, I used to watch your show all the time! I even had your doll!

                    FAN #4
                (Handing Marilyn paper)
Oooh! I can't believe this! Can I get your autograph Nikki?

All About Marilyn

FLASH! Camera phone goes off. FLASH! Marilyn smiles, signs the girl's paper. FLASH! She feels the spotlight on her. FLASH! She doesn't like it. FLASH! She looks past the barricades down the street towards cars. FLASH! She plans to get away as—

FLASH! Another camera goes off. FLASH! Young adults act like little kids again seeing their childhood hero. FLASH! Marilyn leads the extras away from the production signing as many autographs as she can. FLASH! The guards see what she's doing and try to help control the crowd. FLASH! FLASH! FLASH! Cameras all over the place go off. It feels like 1994 again as Marilyn passes—

INT. TABATHA'S TRAILER – MORNING

A luxury suite on wheels. Tabatha in her bathrobe and Ugg boots is snorting lines of meth off a mirror underneath a coffee table plastered with tabloids open to pages of articles featuring her. Her Assistant and Bodyguard struggle to get her ready for today's shoot.

          ASSISTANT
Come on Tabatha, you have a shoot in five minutes. Lay off that shit-

Tabatha cuts a cold glare at her assistant.

          TABATHA
Say one more thing and I'll fire your ass.

          ASSISTANT
Tabatha-

          TABATHA
Shut the fuck up and get my wardrobe ready.

Tabatha's resigned assistant sighs and reaches for the clothes lying on the sofa when they hear the commotion-

And Tabatha hurries over to the window to see—

Marilyn signing autographs. High and pissed, Tabatha lights a cigarette and asks–

>TABATHA
>What the fuck is that Nikki bitch doing on my set?

>BODYGUARD
>It looks like she's leaving. Let her go.

>TABATHA
>Leaving? Why is she on my fucking set in the first fuckin' place?

>ASSISTANT
>She's friends with the director-

Tabatha loses it. She extinguishes her cigarette on her assistant's lapel.

>TABATHA
>No she's not making her comeback on my movie-

>ASSISTANT
>Tabatha calm down-

>TABATHA
>No-

Tabatha storms from the window; her bodyguard and her assistant follow her as she rushes–

EXT. 3800 WILSHIRE BOULEVARD – MORNING

Out of the trailer and bulls her way through the extras. She grabs Marilyn–

All About Marilyn

TABATHA
JUST WHO THE HELL DO YOU THINK
YOU ARE COMING ON MY MOVIE!

MARILYN
I'm just trying to get out of here—

TABATHA
No, you brought your washed up ass here to
take my job—

MARILYN
I don't know what you're talking about—

TABATHA
I saw you talking to the director—

Marilyn notices the glassy look in Tabatha's eyes. She's seen it before. Meth.

MARILYN
You're high. Go sleep it off.

Tabatha can't hear reason. Drugs have her paranoid.

TABATHA
Bitch, don't tell me what to do. It's not All
About Nikki around here—

MARILYN
Don't make a scene—

TABATHA
THIS ISN'T YOUR MOVIE!

SLAP! Tabatha backhands Marilyn across the face. FLASH! FLASH! FLASH! FLASH! FLASH! Cameras explode around Marilyn as she crashes to the ground. FLASH! FLASH! FLASH! FLASH! FLASH! She can't see a thing as—

                    TABATHA
            THIS IS MY MOVIE! MY MOVIE!

CHUT! CHUT! CHUT! CHUT! Tabatha repeatedly kicks and stomps her in the gut and kidneys. Hard. The crowd goes wild.

                    FAN #3
            Oh my God! Tabatha Strong is beating up
            Nikki Desmond!

                    FAN #4
            SOMEBODY GET HER OFF HER!

The guards have their hands full controlling kids trying to get a better shot of the celebrity melee. A worried Clown picks up Marilyn's portfolio, hands it to his friend, and charges over –

                    CLOWN
            Hey lay off Marilyn–

And CRRRUNCH! Tabatha kicks him in the nuts. He crumples to the ground. Tabatha's bodyguard and assistant pull him away. FLASH! FLASH! FLASH! FLASH! FLASH FLASH! FLASH! Cameras explode like fireworks around Marilyn and Tabatha. She coughs up blood as Tabatha grabs a handful of hair and–

SLAM! SLAM! SLAM! Marilyn's head bounces off the asphalt. Some kids cry seeing blood pouring from her forehead.

                    FAN #1
            OH MY GOD SHE'S KILLING NIKKI!

                  CLOWN'S FRIEND
            SOMEBODY HELP HER!

                    FAN #2
            LEAVE HER ALONE!

All About Marilyn

The guards struggle to contain the out of control crowd. Extras are crying and screaming; they can't believe this is happening. A bezerk Tabatha stalks Marilyn like cougar on a wounded fawn. Marilyn staggers up. She realizes she has to fight. She swings and–

CRUNCH! Tabatha's bodyguard slams his fist into Marilyn's jaw. A big guy. Twice her size. Marilyn crashes to the ground. Terrified kids make frantic calls to 911.

> BODYGUARD
> YOU DON'T TOUCH TABATHA!

An enraged Tabatha storms over to the commissary table, grabs a juice bottle, and SMASH! Busts it on the side of the table. She charges towards–

Marilyn who is halfway out of it and about to pass out. Marilyn sees Tabatha on the attack– her eyes grow wide. She lets out a BLOOD CURDLING SCREAM as–

SLASH! Tabatha rakes her across the face with the jagged bottle. The wild crowd grows eerily silent. Tabatha smiles and looks the bloodied Marilyn dead in the eye to tell her–

> TABATHA
> It'll never be All About Nikki again.

CRASH! High Tabatha tosses the bottle over her shoulder, turns, and casually walks back to her trailer. Her bodyguard follows. A battered Marilyn slumps to the ground where–

CUT TO:

MARILYN'S POV

The world is a blur. Marilyn faintly hears KIDS CHATTERING, GARETT'S CRIES, HEAVY FOOTSTEPS, and an AMBULANCE SIREN in the distance. The last thing she hears before everything turns black–

> GIRL
> (Wailing)
> OH MY GOD! NIKKI'S DEAD! NIKKI'S DEAD!

Hours later...

INT. DOWNTOWN LOS ANGELES GENERAL HOSPITAL ROOM 1820 – EVENING

MARILYN'S POV

Voices are heard MUMBLING then getting LOUDER and CLEARER. Strangers. Marilyn's eyes flutter open. The view is different, no peripheral perspective. Marilyn's bandaged hand is seen reaching towards her face to feel–

CUT TO:

Her bandaged face. She rubs against gauze as–

DOCTOR ELLIS in scrubs talks to a NURSE. Both in 40s. Both Black. He notices–

> DOCTOR
> (Taking Marilyn's hand)
> You don't want to touch those.

Marilyn looks around. She sees white curtains on the windows, a TV mounted on the wall. She feels sheets, pillows, and cold steel rails. She realizes she's in a hospital bed.

> MARILYN
> How...how'd I get here?

> DOCTOR
> You suffered a concussion and several facial lacerations Ms. Marie.

All About Marilyn

MARILYN

Tabatha—

NURSE

It looks like she doesn't have any brain damage.

DOCTOR

I'll wait for the MRI.

MARILYN

Why? Why is my face so bandaged for a few cuts?

DOCTOR

You just came out of surgery. There are over three hundred stitches in your face.

The Nurse puts her head down. She can't bear to think about what she's seen in the ER. Marilyn panics and tears at her bandages—

DOCTOR

I told you not to touch those!

MARILYN

I have to see—

NURSE

Ms. Marie— stop!

MARILYN

I HAVE TO SEE!

Marilyn sees the mirror in a nearby—

BATHROOM

And jumps out of bed ripping at her bandages. Doctor Ellis and the Nurse grab at her, but she slips by them into the—

BATHROOM

Cramped like a broom closet. Marilyn locks the door and frantically tears at her bandages. BAM! BAM! BAM! Fists heard pounding, doorknob jerking, Doctor Ellis making pleas as–

Marilyn sees her forehead in the mirror. Tears flow as bandages are pulled away to reveal–

Networks of stitches all over her swollen red, scarred face. Baseball like patterns. Marilyn's cries turn into wails. She falls to her knees on the bathroom floor when–

CRRRRUNCH! Orderlies bust through the door. They drag sobbing Marilyn out of the bathroom–

BACK TO ROOM 1820

And get her back into bed. A screaming, sobbing Marilyn keeps putting her hands to her face. Two orderlies hold her down as–

                NURSE
GET THOSE RESTRAINTS ON NOW!

              DOCTOR
30 CCS's OF THE SEDATIVE STAT!

Two more orderlies tie straps to Marilyn's wrists and ankles. She struggles–

As the Nurse prepares the sedative. She grabs Marilyn's arm and injects. Her tense body goes limp as–

                                        CUT TO:

MARILYN'S POV

Everything goes black again.

DISSOLVE TO:

All About Marilyn

INT. SHAYLA'S HOUSE KITCHEN – NIGHT

A big top of the line kitchen in a Burbank suburb. Shayla is cooking and surfing the net while her husband TERRENCE, 35, plays with their son THOMAS, 4, at the kitchen table. She's multitasking well until–

INSERT

An IM pops up on the computer screen. It says it's about Marilyn with a link to MySpace. Shay clicks the link–

To a series of pictures on a blog of Marilyn in sequence. The shots go from her posing with the Clown and his friend, to a fan feeding frenzy, to an altercation with Tabatha, and a final haunting photo of a bloodied Marilyn lying on the ground. A paragraph above the pictures is titled: "R.I.P. NIKKI DESMOND" and details how Tabatha Strong killed her. Seeing her best friend's obituary–

BACK TO THE KITCHEN

Shay holds back tears. Thomas is about to look, but Terrence notices and takes his son out of the room. Shay grabs the cordless phone and calls–

INT. SABRINA'S OFFICE – NIGHT

Sabrina who is working feverishly on the phone and the computer when BEEEP! The intercom beeps–

          RECEPTIONIST
          (On speaker)
Sabrina, Shayla Sims on line one. She says it's an emergency.

Sabrina hits line one and inquires-

          SABRINA
What's going on Shay?

SHAYLA
(On phone)
Bri, the kids on MySpace are saying Tabatha Strong killed Marilyn on the set of her latest movie. You know what's going on?

SABRINA
Something happened to Marilyn?

SHAYLA
(On phone)
I've seen some pictures of her on some MySpace pages, but they say there's video of what happened. I'm going on YouTube right now.

Sabrina types in www.youtube.com on her computer. Dozens of thumbnails of Marilyn's disfigurement with various titles are next to thumbnails of All About Nikki episodes. Sabrina uploads the video and plays it–

SABRINA
Oh My God. Marilyn.

SHAYLA
(On phone)
You seeing what I'm seeing?

SABRINA
Oh my God. What happened to Marilyn?

SHAYLA
(On phone)
The kids say she was on the set of SELL OUT signing autographs–

SABRINA
I didn't book her on that job–

All About Marilyn

SHAYLA
(On phone)
Maybe she got it on her own–

SABRINA
No, Marilyn can't book jobs without an agent– Oh God.

Sabrina peers up as the receptionist walks in with two L.A.P.D. officers. She's scared to death.

SHAYLA
(On phone)
What's going on Bri?

SABRINA
Shay, I'm going to have to call you back. The police are here.

Sabrina hangs up. The officers state their business.

OFFICER #1
Sabrina Lowenstein? We were told you were the agent representing Marilyn Marie.

SABRINA
What happened to her?

OFFICER #2
She suffered a concussion and several lacerations to her face in an altercation with Tabatha Strong.

SABRINA
Altercation? It's not like Marilyn to fight–

OFFICER #1
All we know is what's written in the reports Ma'am.

SABRINA
Is she all right? All that blood–

OFFICER #2
She's in General Hospital. Room 1820.

SABRINA
When can I see her?

OFFICER #1
Tomorrow.

The Officers leave. Sabrina studies the picture of Marilyn on her desk. She's somber as she punches in Shayla's number–

SABRINA
Shay? She's in General. She's alive.

SHAYLA
(On phone)
Thank God.

SABRINA
I'm going to see her tomorrow. I'll let you know what happened.

DISSOLVE TO:

INT. GENERAL HOSPITAL ROOM 1820 – AFTERNOON

MARILYN'S POV

Marilyn's eyes flutter open. She stirs, gestures–

And looks down at the restraints, then towards the door. The Nurse stands there to tell her–

NURSE
You have a visitor Ms. Marie.

All About Marilyn

CUT TO:

Ava slinking from behind the doorway. She keeps her distance as— Marilyn glares at her.

                    AVA
    Marilyn—

                  MARILYN
    You're fired.

                    AVA
    No, we don't have a contract. In lieu of yesterday's events I feel you're not right for my list. So I'm going to have to withdraw my offer of representation.

Ava walks over to Marilyn's bed. Marilyn clenches fists as she leans over to tell her—

                    AVA
    Tell anyone I was involved yesterday and I'll sue you.

Ava scurries out. The Nurse is about to tend to Marilyn as—

Lori walks in. She prepares to make a speech. Marilyn glares at her.

                    LORI
    Ms. Marie, the members of the Board have taken a vote regarding your residence at Serenity Towers. After yesterday's events we feel you aren't the right kind of tenant for our community.

Marilyn's fists clench tighter as Lori places the eviction notice on the bed. The Nurse is dismayed.

LORI
You'll be recompensed fair market value on the buyout of your apartment.

Lori walks out. The Nurse looks down at the restraints and sympathizes. She'd love to let her loose. Instead she eases the bed up into a sitting position and turns on the TV.

NURSE
Bitches. One day that shit is going to come back to them. God don't like ugly.

MARILYN
Then he must love me. Three hundred stitches?

NURSE
I've seen a lot of shit in the 15 years I've been here. Shotgun wounds, mutilations, crazy shit. I ain't never seen a butchering like what that white girl did to you.

MARILYN
How bad is it?

NURSE
Thank God your face is still attached to your body.

MARILYN
How long am I going to be tied up?

NURSE
Until the Doctor feels you won't be a threat to yourself.

MARILYN
I'm not going to kill myself. You can tell the doctor he can stop hiding the scalpels.

All About Marilyn

The Nurse laughs.

> **NURSE**
> You know, you're all right Marilyn. I could see myself hanging out with you.

Marilyn and the Nurse connect. The conversation is cut short— two men in black designer business suits walk into hospital room like they own it. AN OLDER MARTIN ROSENTHAL, 57, and HIRAM SILVERSTEIN, 68. Hollywood power players.

> **MARTIN**
> We heard Ms. Marie is taking visitors. Could we have a moment alone with her?

The Nurse looks down at the restraints. She doesn't want to leave a friend. Hiram glares at her; Marilyn waves her out. Martin closes the door and turns off the TV.

> **MARTIN**
> Good afternoon Ms. Marie. I'm Martin Rosenthal and this is my client Hiram Silverstein. We represent the production of SELL OUT and Apex Studios.

> **MARILYN**
> I know who you are. Small world isn't it?

Hiram recognizes Marilyn's voice and grimaces.

> **HIRAM**
> That it is. We'd like to apologize for Ms. Strong's actions yesterday.

> **MARILYN**
> Why isn't she in here apologizing herself?

MARTIN
Er– she's been detained. But she's deeply sorry for what she's done to you.

Marilyn sees through the song and dance.

MARILYN
So, she's in rehab.

HIRAM
We want you to know Tabatha Strong is going to be a major star with us.

MARILYN
So was I. I'm still pressing charges.

HIRAM
No charges were filed. No charges are going to be filed.

MARILYN
She butchered me–

MARTIN
You should admit your culpability–

Marilyn channels the too raw for TV version of Nikki Desmond.

MARILYN
What culpability do I have? I was doing a job–

HIRAM
Witnesses say you were signing autographs and taking pictures while trespassing on the set of our production–

All About Marilyn

> MARILYN
> I was doing a job my agent booked. Your junkie and her ape nearly beat me half to death and almost ripped off my damn face! I should sue you for all–

No one ever talks to Hiram Silverstien like that. He grabs Marilyn from her hospital bed. She struggles, her fists clench in restraints. They have an intense staredown–

> HIRAM
> You need to understand it's not All About Nikki anymore–

> MARILYN
> It won't be about Tabatha in five years either–

> HIRAM
> You think this is a joke! Your little stunt cost us a day of production! We had to pay all those extras two thousand dollars apiece to shut them up! I lost close to five million dollars thanks to you!

Hiram's tough talk doesn't scare Marilyn. Martin feels the tension. It's getting personal–

> MARTIN
> Hiram, let her go.

A frustrated Hiram lets Marilyn go and walks away as–

> HIRAM
> Dammit, we're going to be a week behind schedule thanks to this washed up cunt–

Martin gets back to business.

MARTIN
As my client stated Ms. Marie, we have a lot invested in this production. Now we're really sorry about what happened to you, but–

MARILYN
You don't want me to file charges against Tabatha.

HIRAM
We want this to go away.

MARILYN
No, you want me to go away.

MARTIN
We're prepared to offer you compensation for your losses–

The door opens. Sabrina storms in with Doctor Ellis. The strong-arm session ends. They heard most of it.

SABRINA
What kind of compensation are you prepared to give my client?

HIRAM
And you are–

SABRINA
Sabrina Lowenstein, Marilyn Marie's attorney.

MARTIN
Apex Studios and Sell Out Productions are prepared to pay for all Ms. Marie's medical bills, reconstructive surgery, relocation costs, pain and suffering, provided she doesn't press charges on Ms. Strong, doesn't seek any civil

penalties from her or our studios, and she doesn't talk about what happened yesterday.

SABRINA
You're asking my client to give up a lot.

MARTIN
We have a lot riding on this production. It's our tentpole film for the summer. We can't afford any delays.

SABRINA
My client has a lot–

Marilyn wants it to end. She gestures to Sabrina–

MARILYN
I'll prepare a proposal of my terms. You can review it and get back to me.

The strong-arm session has pissed off Doctor Ellis. He storms over to Marilyn and cuts off bandages–

DOCTOR
Gentlemen, do you have kids?

HIRAM
I have two.

MARTIN
I have three.

DOCTOR
Then you better pray to God no one ever does this to them.

Doctor Ellis reveals Marilyn's swollen, scarred, stitched up face. Martin is almost in tears. Hiram feels guilty about earlier–

MARTIN
We'll get to work on that settlement proposal Ms. Marie. Again, we're very, very sorry.

The men dart out of room embarrassed about their behavior. Doctor Ellis undoes the restraints. Marilyn gets out of bed and stretches.

DOCTOR
I'm going to have to put that dressing back on.

MARILYN
(Hops on edge of bed)
Okay.

Sabrina examines Marilyn's face as Doctor Ellis prepares the gauze. She chokes back tears.

SABRINA
My God.

MARILYN
I lost it when I saw it myself. How'd you find out?

SABRINA
It's all over the Internet. Kids are going crazy in the chat rooms and the message boards. I didn't believe it was this bad.

MARILYN
I take it the mainstream media squashed the story.

SABRINA
The networks and the papers haven't said a word about what happened to you.

All About Marilyn

MARILYN
Figures. Apex Studios parent company Viacorp owns most of L.A.'s TV stations and newspapers. They don't want a bad word said about their precious Tabatha Strong.

Dr. Ellis is shocked at what he hears.

DOCTOR
That's no way to treat you.

SABRINA
That's business in Hollywood.

DOCTOR
I thought this room would be flooded with cards and letters from fans today for somebody like you—

MARILYN
Publicists usually set those up. I haven't had one of those since 1998.

SABRINA
It costs money to get attention in this town. You don't have it no one cares.

DOCTOR
That sucks.

MARILYN
That's showbiz.

DOCTOR
If I were you I'd make sure that crazy white bitch was put under a jailhouse. I wouldn't take some settlement—

MARILYN
I'm not doing it for her Doc.

DOCTOR
Then why are you giving up?

MARILYN
A friend of mine wrote SELL OUT. It took him twelve years to get his greenlight. I don't want to cost him his big break.

Dr. Ellis brims with pride. He wants to hug Marilyn but holds off. He continues wrapping bandages. Marilyn's face is almost covered again as he tells her–

DOCTOR
Julia was right about you. You're all right Ms. Marie.

SABRINA
She's a sweetheart.

MARILYN
What's the prognosis Doc? How bad is it?

Doctor Ellis puts his head down. He doesn't want to tell this to a friend.

DOCTOR
Bad. Even though there was no muscle or nerve damage, a lot of the lacerations cut deep into the epidermis. Without major plastic surgery there's going to be permanent scarring.

Marilyn clenches her fist, takes a deep breath, and sucks it up.

All About Marilyn

SABRINA
How long before she can go under the knife again?

DOCTOR
The skin has to heal completely before any more medical trauma is induced.

MARILYN
How long before these stitches come out?

DOCTOR
It'll be a week at least. Like I said, the skin has to heal.

MARILYN
Thanks Doc.

DOCTOR
My name is Ellis. If you need anything buzz the front desk.

Dr. Ellis walks out and closes the door. Marilyn gets up and walks over to the window. Sabrina follows as Marilyn stares at her reflection. Under the bandages she sees her true self for the first time.

SABRINA
You did a wonderful thing for Garrett.

MARILYN
He doesn't deserve to suffer.

SABRINA
Neither do you.

MARILYN
This is my fault. You told me to get out. I didn't listen–

                    SABRINA
Marilyn, it's not your fault. You were just on a job—

                    MARILYN
I took that job because I was scared.

Sabrina is disheartened seeing the truth about Marilyn.

                    SABRINA
Marilyn—

                    MARILYN
You were right about me. I was scared. So scared of moving on I played the part of the struggling actress for twelve years.

                    SABRINA
Marilyn, I didn't mean it like that—

                    MARILYN
Sure you did. You loved me enough to tell me the truth. You didn't want to see me drown like Tabatha.

Sabrina is brought to tears hearing the truth. First time she's cried in years.

                    SABRINA
I didn't want to see this happen to you—

                    MARILYN
It had to happen Bri. Now I can't pretend anymore. I don't have Nikki Desmond's mask to hide behind, no Downtown apartment to surround myself with relics of the past. I have to face the ugly reality my life has become.

All About Marilyn

Sabrina is a mess. Marilyn reaches out to comfort her. Her smile makes Sabrina feel better.

> MARILYN
> Come on Bri, don't fall apart on me. I need your help to do this one last job.

Sabrina composes herself.

> SABRINA
> I've never seen this side of you Marilyn. So determined–

> MARILYN
> I'm not scared anymore.

> SABRINA
> So you're off the boat?

> MARILYN
> I'm swimming.

> SABRINA
> The studio smells your blood. They're going to send their sharks after us.

> MARILYN
> I'm in the mood for sushi.

Marilyn sits on the side of the bed and Sabrina opens up her briefcase. Marilyn grabs a legal pad next to her headshot and writes–

> MARILYN
> This is what I want you to take to them…

DISSOLVE TO:

INT. GENERAL HOSPITAL ROOM 1820 – AFTERNOON

Days pass. Marilyn's face is still bandaged. She's sitting up in bed sipping on a milkshake watching TV when–

The Clown in T-shirt and jeans walks into the room with a nervous look on his face. He carries Marilyn's battered portfolio with him. She clicks off the TV and smiles at him as he approaches.

                CLOWN
   You dropped this.

Marilyn takes the portfolio and unzips it. Everything is there.

              MARILYN
   Wow. I never thought I'd see this again. My
   whole life was in there–

The Clown gets choked up. Marilyn takes his hand. She gestures and he sits on the edge of the bed. The kid is almost in tears.

                CLOWN
   I– I'm really sorry about what happened–

Marilyn consoles him with a kind look.

              MARILYN
   Look, it wasn't your fault–

                CLOWN
   But if I hadn't called you out–

              MARILYN
   Somebody else would have. Don't beat
   yourself up about it. It's just nice to know I
   still have one fan left in the world.

The Clown's spirits are lifted by the joke.

All About Marilyn

              CLOWN
I didn't see anything about you on the news–

              MARILYN
Viacorp, Apex Studios' parent company and the owner of three local L.A. TV stations squashed the story.

              CLOWN
Well, my friends and I put some stuff up on MySpace.

              MARILYN
That was you? Man, if it wasn't for you my friends wouldn't even know I was in here.

The Clown feels proud about his good deed. Marilyn takes out her pen and pulls one of her headshots out of the portfolio. The Clown lights up.

              MARILYN
I never did get your name–

              CLOWN
Adam. My name is Adam.

              MARILYN
      (Writing autograph)
Well, Adam, I hope this inspires you more than the show ever did.

Adam looks down at the autograph that reads: "To Adam– Nikki Desmond's number one fan and Marilyn's friend." He'll cherish this for the rest of his life.

              CLOWN
Thanks Marilyn.

                    MARILYN
        Break a leg.

Marilyn shakes Adam's hand. He smiles as he leaves. On his way out he bumps into–

A casually dressed Shayla and Lucia carrying shopping bags. Marilyn jumps out of bed and hugs them tightly.

                    SHAYLA
        We got you some stuff.

Lucy closes the door. Shay hands her the bags.

Marilyn smiles appreciatively as she takes out black silk pajamas, a black silk robe, black terrycloth slippers, and toiletries.

                    MARILYN
        Thanks guys.

                    LUCIA
        How you been holding up?

                    MARILYN
        My face is in stitches, my mind in one piece.

                    SHAYLA
        I heard from Bri about you losing your apartment. I'm sorry.

                    MARILYN
        Didn't want to live around those snobs anyway.

Marilyn grabs her portfolio off the bed, takes out her keys, and tosses them to Lucy–

All About Marilyn

MARILYN
Look out for my apartment Lucy. Water the plants, vacuum the carpets–

LUCIA
Make sure no one moves your stuff out while you're gone. Your tub still has those jets right?

MARILYN
Don't go crazy.

LUCIA
Don't worry, su casa es mi casa.

SHAYLA
You know when you get out of here you can still stay with us–

MARILYN
You know how Terrence feels about me–

SHAYLA
Honey, Terrence changed his mind when he saw those videos on the Internet.

MARILYN
He still calling me a freeloader?

SHAYLA
You know progress with Terrence is a slow process.

The women laugh.

MARILYN
So, when are you moving out to the East Coast Shay?

SHAYLA
I'm headed out to New York to close on the brownstone next week. So by the end of the month we should be out there.

MARILYN
I don't know how long I'm going to be here. I'll try to keep in touch.

Shayla opens her purse, scribbles on a notepad, and hands it to Marilyn.

SHAYLA
That's my address. If you're ever in New York look us up.

MARILYN
I'll definitely do that.

Marilyn unties her hospital gown and throws it across the bed. Shay and Lucy are shocked seeing the bruises on Marilyn's nude body.

LUCIA
Dios Mio.

MARILYN
What? It's just us in here like the locker room at Jim's–

SHAYLA
(Examining bruises)
What'd she do to you?

MARILYN
What do you think Tabatha did to me Shay? She beat the crap out of me.

Marilyn smiles at Shay and Lucy as she changes into pajamas. They notice something different about her on the inside.

All About Marilyn

LUCIA
Something about you has changed.

MARILYN
I'm not acting anymore.

The door opens. Sabrina, Hiram, and Martin walk into the room along with Dr. Ellis and a Photographer. Marilyn sits on the bed, grabs a pad off the tray table, and crosses her legs. She's as cool as December.

SHAYLA
Well, I better get back home. I need to pack. Come on Lucy.

MARILYN
I'll see you in New York Shay.

Shay and Lucy leave the room. Marilyn gets down to business as—

MARTIN
Ms. Marie, I reviewed the proposal you had Ms. Lowenstein submit to us. Some of your requests were a little bizarre—

Doctor Ellis peels off the bandages. Hiram and Martin are mortified as Marilyn brushes her hair.

MARILYN
This is how I want the settlement broken down.

HIRAM
You want us to take a portrait photograph of your face in its current state? A ten percent donation of the value of all settlement earnings, a brand new top-of-the-line computer, office furniture, and a new fully

equipped Dodge Sprinter donated to Burbank Baptist Church?

MARILYN
Tabatha probably asks you for crazier stuff. She out of rehab yet?

MARTIN
She's fine. She's filming SELL OUT as we speak. She wanted you to have this letter of apology–

Marilyn takes the letter, rips it in half, and throws it over her shoulders. She knows an assistant wrote it.

MARILYN
Great.

HIRAM
We want to pay for all your reconstructive surgery in addition to your medical bills–

MARILYN
No limit on cost.

MARTIN
No limit on cost.

Doctor Ellis smiles. $!

HIRAM
Where do you plan to live after all this?

MARILYN
I take it I'm no longer welcome in Los Angeles.

All About Marilyn

MARTIN
We just want a sense of how much your relocation costs will be.

Marilyn looks across table at Shayla's address.

MARILYN
Harlem. I want a one-bedroom apartment there like the one I used to own here.

HIRAM
Those New York apartments go for at least a half-million dollars now—

MARILYN
What was the fair market value of my old apartment Bri?

SABRINA
A one-bedroom luxury apartment in Downtown Burbank currently goes for $1.5 to $2 million dollars.

MARILYN
A half-million sounds like pocket change compared to the $10 million you're paying Tabatha to put up her nose.

Hiram is nauseous looking at Marilyn's face. He wants this to end.

HIRAM
(Looking at Martin)
I think I know someone with a property out there he wants to sell—

MARTIN
We'll get the deed out to you ASAP Ms. Marie. Now about your furniture—

MARILYN
With the exception of my personal effects and my All About Nikki memorabilia, I'm donating it to Burbank Baptist Church. You'll buy me all new furniture and have it delivered to the apartment.

MARTIN
No problem.

MARILYN
In addition, you'll pay the moving expenses and my travel expenses. I want a private jet whenever I need it.

HIRAM
No problem. About financial compensation for your pain and suffering you didn't determine–

MARILYN
Hard to say what it's worth. I had what, at least ten, fifteen good years left on my acting career–

HIRAM
You were washed up before this–

MARILYN
The folks on YouTube don't think so. My disfiguring at Tabatha's hands was the most downloaded video all last week next to old All About Nikki episodes–

HIRAM
We pulled those videos–

All About Marilyn

SABRINA
At least a million people downloaded them before they were pulled. Besides, they're still being file shared on Kazaa, LimeWire, BitTorrent, and they're still being posted all over MySpace and YouTube. Do you really want to take this to trial?

HIRAM
Those kids aren't going to be on a jury—

MARILYN
You go to trial and I guarantee you their Middle American parents will never buy another Tabatha Strong product again.

MARTIN
She's got us there. We can't afford any further damage to Tabatha's brand—

Hiram wants this business done. Marilyn's face is scaring the hell out of him.

HIRAM
Fine In addition to your— requests we're prepared to offer you a cash payment of two million dollars to cover pain and suffering. We'll also pay all legal fees.

SABRINA
Two million? What about lost wages?

MARTIN
Ms. Marie wasn't permanently disabled by the assault. With retraining, we believe she can find comparable employment in another field.

SABRINA
She lost her career—

Sabrina is worried. Marilyn sees possibilities.

                    MARILYN
        It's fine Bri. Gentlemen I accept your offer.

Hiram is glad it's over. He can look down.

                    HIRAM
        We'll work out the details of the settlement
        contract with your attorney.

Hiram extends his hand. Marilyn shakes it. Deal is sealed.

                    MARILYN
        If that's business gentlemen, I'd like to take
        this picture. I showered and got dressed up
        for it.

The Photographer gets into position. Marilyn puts on a movie star smile. FLASH! FLASH! FLASH! Hiram and Martin are queasy seeing the movie star smile around stitches.

                    MARTIN
        Good day Ms. Marie.

Marilyn lets Nikki take a parting swipe.

                    MARILYN
        Oh and Hiram?

                    HIRAM
        Yes?

                    MARILYN
        If you ever call me a cunt again I'll kick you in
        your nuts so hard they'll be in your throat.

An embarrassed Hiram scurries out of room with Martin and the photographer.

All About Marilyn

Doctor Ellis is impressed. He hasn't seen legal wrangling like that. Ever.

ELLIS
Which one of you was the attorney again?

SABRINA
I'm trying to figure that out myself. Did you even need me?

MARILYN
I just know what I want Bri. Am I going to need the bandages again Ellis?

ELLIS
The swelling has gone down. No signs of infection. I'll put em' on later.

SABRINA
I still think you could have gotten more–

MARILYN
God doesn't like greedy Bri.

SABRINA
At least I'll get some billable hours out of this. Going out to be with Shayla?

MARILYN
At least I know I'll have one friend in New York.

ELLIS
Are you going to be okay in Harlem?

MARILYN
I'll probably be right at home Doc. So how am I doing?

ELLIS
Everything is healing up nicely, so I can schedule the stitches to come out soon.

MARILYN
Great. How long am I going to be here after that?

Ellis looks at the eviction notice on table. He wants to help her out.

ELLIS
Due to the extensive nature of your injuries, I need to do further observation. Call in a plastic surgeon, dermatology specialist. We'll have to move you into a suite upstairs to facilitate your better care.

SABRINA
You're going to milk the studio for all it's worth.

ELLIS
They gave me no limit on expenditures.

MONTAGE

Months pass. We see:

- a) Marilyn in surgery getting stitches out,
- b) Face bandaged.
- c) Bandages removed.
- d) Scars healing.
- e) The Reverend and Lucia surprised by a red Dodge Sprinter, office furniture and computer donated to Burbank Baptist Church.
- f) Lucia looking at a card under the windshield wiper saying, "Thanks for everything" signed by Marilyn. She smiles.
- g) Sabrina in her office reviewing the settlement contract. She calls Marilyn in–

All About Marilyn

INT. LOS ANGELES GENERAL HOSPITAL SUITE 3430 – AFTERNOON

A nice room, almost like an apartment with a private bath, a bed with a headboard and footboard, cable box, and a private phone. Marilyn sits on the side of bed clad in black silk pajamas watching TV as she picks up the phone–

> SABRINA
> (On phone)
> Marilyn, the studio sent over the final draft of the settlement contract. Most of it looks good. They want to know when you want to sign–

> MARILYN
> You can bring them over today Bri. I've got a consultation with the plastic surgeon in a couple of minutes.

> SABRINA
> (On phone)
> I'll be there in an hour.

Marilyn hangs up as–

Dr. Ellis and DR. DELIA SAUNDERS, 47, a black medical professional on the top of her game walk into the suite. Marilyn smiles, turns off the TV, and gets up.

> ELLIS
> Marilyn, this is Dr. Delia Saunders, the plastic surgeon I was telling you about.

> DELIA
> (Extending hand)
> It's a pleasure to meet you Ms. Marie.

MARILYN
(Shaking hand)
Nice to meet you Dr. Saunders. You think you can fix this wreck?

Ellis laughs at the joke. Delia examines Marilyn's face. She sees possibilities.

DELIA
Based on the dermatology tests you're the best candidate for this kind of reconstructive surgery.

MARILYN
What kind of face can I expect to have at after this?

DELIA
Based on the pattern of the healing scars, I can restore your face close to what it looked like before the assault.

Ellis smiles. He did a good job.

ELLIS
When can we schedule surgery?

DELIA
She's healing up nicely, so I'd say in about three weeks.

MARILYN
And I was getting used to seeing this face in the mirror every morning.

ELLIS
I'll set everything up.

All About Marilyn

Ellis and Delia leave. Sabrina walks in carrying a briefcase. Marilyn sits on the edge of the bed. Sabrina opens her briefcase and pulls out a binder—

SABRINA
How'd it go with the plastic surgeon?

MARILYN
In three weeks I'll be on my way to a new face.

SABRINA
That's wonderful!

MARILYN
I don't know. I think I'm going to miss this one.

SABRINA
You actually like looking like this—

MARILYN
I actually like myself now.

Sabrina is worried. She thinks Marilyn is losing it.

MARILYN
So what's been going on the legal front Bri?

SABRINA
They sent pictures of the new apartment. It's the Lenox Terrace, on 135th and Lenox.

Sabrina opens the binder to reveal pictures. Marilyn likes what she sees.

MARILYN
The address isn't too far from Shay's place. It looks like it's comfortable—

SABRINA
The studio used their set decorator to furnish your apartment. Everything is brand new.

MARILYN
Nice to see they're acting in good faith. What's the maintenance fee?

SABRINA
$875 a month. Utilities included.

MARILYN
I can swing that once I find a job.

SABRINA
I still think you could have gotten more–

MARILYN
I just want enough money for college.

SABRINA
I know. God doesn't like greedy.

MARILYN
What's going on with the sale of my old apartment?

SABRINA
The sale is nowhere near closing.

MARILYN
How long is it going to take? It's been six months already–

SABRINA
The Tower Board is dragging its feet. I can't even get anyone on the phone–

All About Marilyn

MARILYN

Lori and her cronies are trying to stick it to me.

SABRINA

You could stay with me after you get out of the hospital–

MARILYN

No, I've got to go to New York. Hiram and his studio cronies will make life impossible for us both if I stay in L.A.

SABRINA

Don't worry about me. I can handle a couple of studio sharks. You need a place to stay.

MARILYN

I'll figure something out. You tell them I'll be signing after I get my new face.

SABRINA

I'll do everything I can to expedite the money from the sale of your old co-op.

MARILYN

Thanks Bri.

Sabrina gives Marilyn a hug, shuts her briefcase and walks out. She's worried about her friend.

Marilyn walks over to mirror and smiles. She likes what she sees as she–

MONTAGE

a) Changes into a hospital gown,
b) Delia makes marks on her face,
c) Is rolled into the operating room,

d) Goes under anesthesia,
e) Thumbs up from Delia in the operating room.
f) Marilyn's face wrapped in bandages as she sits up in bed reading Variety. The headline reads: "TICKETS WILL SELL OUT ON JULY 4 WEEKEND". Marilyn puts down the magazine, smiles and–
g) Walks back in front of the mirror where there's–

INT. LOS ANGELES GENERAL HOSPITAL SUITE 3430 – AFTERNOON

A big celebration, with cake and decorations. It's Marilyn's 35th birthday. Sabrina and Ellis are present as–

Delia cuts and peels off the bandages. We see Marilyn's forehead, eyes focused. Skin is smooth. The bridge of the nose is revealed, and then her cheeks, and chin. Everyone reacts to seeing–

Marilyn's smile growing wide. More beautiful than ever. Sabrina notices something different. Something about those eyes and that smile.

DELIA
(Holding headshot up)
She looks just like her headshot.

ELLIS
Better than her headshot.

DELIA
I wish I could add this one to my after picture book.

MARILYN
The settlement contract doesn't say anything about a personal photo.

DELIA
I'll go get my camera.

All About Marilyn

Delia and Ellis leave the room. Sabrina closes the door and expresses her concerns. Marilyn gets some cake.

SABRINA
So what are you going to do once you get out of the hospital?

MARILYN
Go home, pack my stuff, head to the hairdresser–

SABRINA
Hairdresser?

MARILYN
Yeah. I'm not wearing Nikki Desmond's hair to New York. Maybe I'll dye it black–

SABRINA
What's with all the black lately?

MARILYN
The black is me saying I'm not a character anymore.

SABRINA
Marilyn, are you okay?

MARILYN
I'm fine.

SABRINA
It's just that you've been different these past couple of months.

MARILYN
I'm not acting anymore.

SABRINA
What are you acting like?

Marilyn explains.

MARILYN
Ever since my acting career fell apart I've had to hold my feelings in to keep it together.

SABRINA
I always thought you came to me with your problems–

MARILYN
I came to you about business stuff like getting rejected at auditions. But I couldn't tell anyone how I felt inside about things–

SABRINA
Things that upset you.

MARILYN
Stuff like getting called Nikki by strangers, hassles at the gym, people just picking at me–

SABRINA
I never knew you were under so much pressure–

MARILYN
Even though the show has been over for years, people still keep reacting to the character they saw on TV, not thinking about how I feel.

SABRINA
So you turn the other cheek.

All About Marilyn

MARILYN
I have to forgive them Bri. They may not know what they're doing but I know they don't know what they're doing.

SABRINA
Projecting Nikki's character onto you.

MARILYN
I think people would lose their minds if they found out how I struggle to pay my bills just like them.

SABRINA
How does this change anything? You have the same face as before–

MARILYN
They saw Nikki die.

SABRINA
They saw you get disfigured–

MARILYN
The last thing I heard a girl say before I passed out that day was Nikki is dead. To the public she's finally gone.

SABRINA
And the studio paid for her funeral.

MARILYN
I feel like I have a ton of bricks lifted off me. I can go on with my life now.

SABRINA
You're free.

MARILYN
Free to be myself.

Dr. Ellis and Dr. Saunders walk in with a digital camera. They close the door, hand Sabrina the camera, and stand next to Marilyn–

FLASH! Big movie star smiles. The party's over when–

KNOCK! KNOCK! KNOCK! Delia saves the picture, slips the camera in her lab coat pocket and opens the door. Hiram and Martin walk into suite ready to close the deal. Martin is floored by Marilyn's beauty.

MARILYN
What brings you by gentlemen?

MARTIN
Wow. Er…we wanted to take a look to see how your reconstructive procedure went.

DELIA
It was a tremendous success. Ms. Marie looks just like her headshot.

MARTIN
Headshot? She looks better than Tabatha. We should have cast her–

Hiram punches Martin in arm. He doesn't want to hear the truth.

HIRAM
That means we can finish business with Ms. Marie today. You doctors can stay. I'll need witnesses to the signing.

Martin walks over to the dresser, opens his briefcase and pulls out the settlement contracts. Marilyn and Sabrina approach him as he pulls back the triplicate contracts and–

All About Marilyn

Marilyn signs the first, second, and then the third copies. Martin hands one to Sabrina, then hands Marilyn her apartment keys and the deed. Hiram smiles. There's something behind this.

MARTIN
Here are the keys to your new apartment at the Lenox Terrace.

MARILYN
Apartment 5A. Great.

MARTIN
We're sending moving trucks to your property on Wednesday. One for your furniture, the other for your personal effects.

SABRINA
When can my client expect to see her cash payment?

HIRAM
That would be five months from now.

All are shocked. SWERVE!

SABRINA
That's not in the contract you sent me–

HIRAM
It's in the settlement contract your client just signed.

SABRINA
What's Marilyn supposed to do for food in New York? Pay her bills?

HIRAM
Look, our money is tied up. We can't afford to pay Ms. Marie until the next fiscal year.

SABRINA
Next fiscal year? That's bullshit–

MARTIN
Ms. Lowenstein, we've acted in good faith. We've paid for Ms. Marie's medical bills, surgery, and honored all her unique requests. We're even paying for her relocation costs.

SABRINA
You just used studio perks to cover the non-cash parts of the compensation.

MARTIN
As far as we're concerned, we are finished doing business with Ms. Marie. She'll get her cash payment on January 3rd of next year.

HIRAM
I just want you to know Ms. Lowenstein, the world premiere of SELL OUT is coming up next Friday. We'd like to have Ms. Marie on a plane to New York by the end of the week.

Sabrina is pissed. Marilyn is cool as December.

MARILYN
I'll be on it.

Martin and Hiram storm out. Coals heaped on their heads.

ELLIS
I was going to release you tomorrow. But I can schedule a few more days of observation–

MARILYN
No Doc, you've done your part. This is where I come in.

All About Marilyn

Marilyn and Sabrina look at each other in the mirror.

                    SABRINA

They got us.

                    MARILYN

They got us good.

                    SABRINA

I should have looked those contracts over again before you signed them–

                    MARILYN

Don't beat yourself up Bri. You acted in good faith. It was all you could do.

                    SABRINA

But you're right back where you started from.

                    MARILYN

The settlement was to make me whole. I was supposed to be back where I started from.

                    SABRINA

But what are you going to do for the next five months?

                    MARILYN

I'll trust God to figure something out.

The next day–

INT. GENERAL HOSPITAL LOBBY – MORNING

Dr. Ellis pushes Marilyn in a wheelchair. Marilyn dressed in an old white fitted blouse, faded blue jeans, and sneakers is wheeled out to-

EXT. STREET – MORNING

The curb where–

Sabrina is waiting for her in her new black Mercedes convertible. Marilyn says goodbye to Ellis, jumps up out of the chair, puts her bag in the trunk, and gets in–

INT. SABRINA'S CAR – MORNING

MOVING

That drives down busy L.A. city streets.

                MARILYN
New car?

                SABRINA
A retirement gift for myself.

                MARILYN
You deserve it.

                SABRINA
The movers will be at your place by ten.

                MARILYN
Yeah, I called Lucy and told her to meet us downstairs.

                              CUT TO:

Sabrina's car hitting the–

FREEWAY EXIT RAMP

Passing by a sign saying "BURBANK". She continues driving downtown towards–

All About Marilyn

SERENITY TOWERS

Where she punches in the code at the security gate then continues down the path into the—

PARKING LOT

Where Sabrina parks in space 3C. Moving trucks are nearby. Lori stops hassling the movers and walks up to them—

>> LORI
> Excuse me, you can't park here. Tenants only. Guests—

>> MARILYN
> It's my parking space until you pay me for it.

Lori takes a second look as they get out of the car.

>> LORI
> Marilyn?

>> MARILYN
> Hi Lori.

>> LORI
> You're moving?

>> MARILYN
> You evicted me.

>> LORI
> You were supposed to set up a schedule with me—

>> MARILYN
> You're here. I'm here. The movers are here. We're on schedule to move.

SABRINA
I'd like to know when you're going to recompense my client for her property—

LORI
The Board is having a hard time raising the funds to buy you out. One and two bedroom apartments aren't too popular on the market these days.

MARILYN
Why don't you just refinance the building?

LORI
We just don't have the resources—

MARILYN
You have 180 days to get me my money or my attorney will be taking you to court. Good day Ms. Lewis.

Lori is left flabbergasted. Marilyn gestures to the movers. Sabrina smiles as they walk into—

INT. SERENITY TOWERS LOBBY – MORNING

Where Lucia and Gregory are waiting for them. They give Marilyn a big hug.

LUCIA
Oh Marilyn— I missed you so much!

MARILYN
I missed you too Lucy. How long have you been waiting?

LUCIA
Ten minutes. Your Tower Board President— Ay Dios Mio.

All About Marilyn

MARILYN
Well, we won't be here long.

The group walks towards the—

ELEVATOR BANK

They ride up to the—

THIRD FLOOR

Marilyn's anticipation builds as Lucia opens Apartment #3C—

INT. MARILYN'S APARTMENT LIVING ROOM – MORNING

Just like she left it. Marilyn directs the movers—

MARILYN
Okay, all the stuff on the walls, the picture frames, and the display case go to New York along with the stuff in the bedroom and the linen closets. The rest is going to the Church.

The movers nod their heads and get to business. The Reverend wants to express his gratitude.

GREGORY
I want to thank you for all the wonderful gifts. We were able to help a lot more people thanks to you.

MARILYN
It was nothing. You've done so much for me over the past couple of years I owed you.

LUCIA
I just wish you could stay here.

> MARILYN
> I wish I could stay too.

Marilyn gets choked up watching framed posters being taken off the wall and bubble wrapped. She can't bear to watch her life being packed up in boxes. She smiles at Lucy as she asks her–

> MARILYN
> Hey Lucy, want to hang out? You can watch me fix my hair and wardrobe–

Lucia lights up.

> LUCIA
> Just like we used to do during Spring Break back in the day.

> MARILYN
> This time it'll be more fun.

Sabrina sees Marilyn's tears and hands her car keys and a credit card.

> SABRINA
> We'll look out for your stuff until you come back.

Marilyn and Lucia leave the apartment. They get in Sabrina's convertible, head down to Rodeo Drive, and park in front of–

INT. MANUEL'S HAIR SALON – MORNING

Early, no one there. Marilyn walks in, gets into a chair, undoes her ponytail, and asks the hairdresser–

> MARILYN
> What can you do with this?

All About Marilyn

                MANUEL
    (Running fingers through hair)
Let me see...

Hours later...

A long shiny, straight black hairdo flows as Marilyn and Lucy walk out of the hairdresser into the next door–

EXT. DESIGNER BOUTIQUE – AFTERNOON

A few moments later Marilyn comes out dressed in black sunglasses, a black boatneck shirt, Capri pants and ballet flats. She and Lucy carry lots of shopping bags. The makeover is complete. Nikki Desmond is no more.

They get into Sabrina's car and drive–

BACK TO SERENITY TOWERS

She and Lucy hurry up to apartment #3C where–

INT. MARILYN'S APARTMENT – EVENING

The door is wide open. The movers packing last of the stuff. Reverend Gregory and Sabrina are laughing exchanging Marilyn stories when–

She makes her entrance in doorway. Everyone is shocked at the sight of the new Marilyn.

                SABRINA
Miss, are you sure you have the right apartment?

                MARILYN
    (Peering under sunglasses)
Bri, you know it's me.

SABRINA
I was just messing with you. I love the new look. The dark hair makes you look like a different person.

MARILYN
Thanks.

Gregory smiles proudly and hugs Marilyn tightly.

GREGORY
I'm going to miss you.

MARILYN
I'll never forget you Reverend.

Lucy smiles and gets one last look at her best friend. Tears well up in her eyes as she hugs her.

LUCIA
You go out there and be the brightest light you can be.

Marilyn breaks the embrace and smiles at her.

MARILYN
I will.

Reverend Gregory and Lucy leave. Marilyn and Sabrina stare out of the picture windows of an empty apartment.

SABRINA
I made sure they took care of your Nikki memorabilia. It'll be on the plane with you tomorrow.

MARILYN
Thanks.

All About Marilyn

SABRINA
Exiled from Hollywood. What a way to end a career.

MARILYN
It's better than going out doing Lifetime movies–

SABRINA
Doing infomercials or posing in Playboy–

MARILYN
Writing some tell-all book denouncing everyone for ruining my life.

Both laugh.

SABRINA
And what would you write about me?

MARILYN
I couldn't say a bad thing about you Bri. You kept me from that fate. At least this way I'm going out on my own terms.

SABRINA
Do you ever think you'll miss the business?

MARILYN
It was fun doing the struggling actress bit, but I don't think I'll miss it. I'm actually looking forward to a life of steady paychecks and brand name groceries.

SABRINA
We made a great team.

MARILYN
Yeah, we did.

SABRINA
You want to stay at my house tonight?

Marilyn looks into Sabrina's eyes. She wants one last night with her before she leaves. Marilyn smiles and tells her–

MARILYN
I did want to get one last look at the Santa Monica Coast.

Both women walk out. Marilyn shuts out the lights and closes the door on Hollywood. The–

NEXT MORNING

EXT. SABRINA'S CAR – MORNING

MOVING

Sabrina's car drives down the freeway. She leaves the off ramp to drive towards–

BOB HOPE AIRPORT

Sabrina in jeans and a chambray shirt pops the trunk. Marilyn dressed in black takes out suitcases and heads to the curb. Sabrina reaches into her purse, counts off $1000–

MARILYN
Put your money away Bri.

SABRINA
This is *your* money. I'll deduct it from your settlement check.

MARILYN
Bri–

All About Marilyn

                    SABRINA
I may be retired, but I'm still your agent. This will get you some groceries.

Marilyn laughs and stuffs the money in her pants pocket.

                    MARILYN
Thanks.

                    SABRINA
Well, I guess this is goodbye.

                    MARILYN
I guess I'll see you in four years.

                    SABRINA
Four years?

                    MARILYN
College graduation Bri. You're definitely going to be there aren't you?

                    SABRINA
I wouldn't miss it for the world.

Both women hug. Sabrina smiles proudly watching Marilyn walk into the terminal with her bags. She knows she'll see her friend again before then. Hours later...

INT. PRIVATE JET – AFTERNOON

MOVING

Marilyn sips on cola as she punches in a number on the jet's phone BRRRING! BRRRRING! The phone picks up–

                    SHAYLA
                    (On phone)
Professor Sims.

                    MARILYN
What's up Shay?

                    SHAYLA
                   (On phone)
MARILYN! OH MY GOD! What's it been–?

                    MARILYN
A year Shay. I'm on the plane headed your way.

                    SHAYLA
                   (On phone)
I know. Sabrina called me. In the middle of a class. Don't you California people know about time zone differentials?

                    MARILYN
I know. Three-hour difference. Nine AM L.A. Time is noon New York time. My flight lands at LaGuardia at four.

                    SHAYLA
                   (On phone)
I'll be there to pick you up.

                    MARILYN
Cool.

Marilyn hangs up the phone as–

The plane begins its descent. It lands and–

Marilyn gets off the plane. She heads into–

INT. LAGUARDIA AIRPORT – AFTERNOON

A busy air hub bustling with action. Across the terminal Marilyn notices–

All About Marilyn

Shayla holding up a sign saying "WELCOME TO NEW YORK MARILYN". Marilyn smiles—

And walks up behind Shayla. Shayla doesn't notice her until—

MARILYN
Boo.

Shayla gets a good look at Marilyn and gives her best friend a hug.

SHAYLA
Marilyn? I didn't recognize you.

MARILYN
You weren't supposed to. How you doing girl?

SHAYLA
Great. What's with all the black? It's summer.

MARILYN
It allows me to disappear.

SHAYLA
Well that's all most people wear around here. I felt so out of place the first few weeks here wearing my pastels.

MARILYN
Have you adjusted to life in the big city?

SHAYLA
A year in I'm just getting used to it.

Shayla checks her watch. Late!

SHAYLA
Oh— I've got to get you back to your apartment. I've got a class coming up at six.

                    MARILYN
I guess that's another New York thing, all this clockwatching.

                    SHAYLA
Yeah. People always have to be someplace at sometime here.

                    MARILYN
You don't have to rush around on my part. I'll get home when I do.

                    SHAYLA
I thought you wanted to rest–

                    MARILYN
I'll do that tomorrow. I want to see where you work.

Shayla smiles. She and Marilyn hurry through terminal out to the–

EXT. LAGUARDIA AIRPORT PARKING LOT – AFTERNOON

Where they pack her bags in the back of Shay's SUV and drive off. The conversation continues in–

INT. SHAYLA'S SUV – EVENING

MOVING

                    MARILYN
So how has it been back on the job stimulating those dangerous minds?

                    SHAYLA
Hectic. But I'm used to it now.

All About Marilyn

MARILYN
I see you've been keeping up on your workouts.

SHAYLA
Well, you know I like looking *foine*. Doesn't hurt that there's a gym across the street from the college.

MARILYN
What are the services like?

SHAYLA
Nothing like Jim's in L.A., but they have most of the circuit training equipment. I usually get a decent workout in after work.

MARILYN
I'll scope it out.

SHAYLA
What's your plan for the next couple of months?

MARILYN
Look at some schools, look for work.

SHAYLA
Y'know I was talking to this professor friend of mine. He might have a job you can do.

MARILYN
What kind of job?

SHAYLA
Modeling.

MARILYN
Shay, I'm out of the business–

SHAYLA

Trust me, this isn't entertainment. He really needs someone to help him out.

MARILYN

Bri told you about my money situation.

SHAYLA

She's just looking out for you. Besides, this guy is nice. He's not going to railroad you.

Shayla's SUV drives downtown to–

EXT. 14th STREET AND FIFTH NEXT SCHOOL CAMPUS – EVENING

A college campus spaced between old factory buildings converted into offices, shops, and apartments. The school buildings have flags on them that state: "THE NEXT SCHOOL FOR THE NEXT GENERATION OF STUDENTS."

An awe-struck Marilyn takes in the sights and sounds of campus life as they park in front of the–

FINE ARTS BUILDING

With a red flag out front. Shayla lets Marilyn in to see–

INT. NEXT SCHOOL FINE ARTS BUILDING LOBBY – EVENING

Lots of student paintings and sculptures on display. Shayla flashes her ID, Marilyn signs in and sticks a guest tag on the breast of her polo shirt. She studies the art displayed on the walls as they walk down corridor to a door stating–

HEAD OF FINE ARTS DEPARTMENT

Shayla opens the door of–

All About Marilyn

INT. FINE ARTS DEPARTMENT OFFICE – EVENING

A neat organized office space with student art hanging on the walls and student sculptures in the bookcase. At his desk typing on the computer is CHRIS CHERRY, 67, an old school brother who loves his job. He lights up at the sight of Shayla–

CHRIS
Shayla, this is a surprise. What brings you by?

SHAYLA
I wanted you to meet my friend. Marilyn, this is Chris Cherry, head of the Fine Arts Department here at the Next School.

CHRIS
(Extending hand)
Marilyn.

MARILYN
(Shaking hand)
Nice to meet you Professor.

CHRIS
Call me Chris. I can't stand titles.

Chris gestures and the ladies have a seat in front of his desk.

SHAYLA
I brought Marilyn by so you could tell her more about the modeling job.

CHRIS
(Pulls out Marilyn's headshot)
Yes, my last model dropped out of school right in the middle of the semester. I've got a figure art class coming up tomorrow and I really need someone to fill in. Shayla tells me you have a modeling background–

MARILYN
I did some print ads back in the mid 90's. I also did a couple of magazine covers.

CHRIS
Could you hold a pose for an extended period of time?

MARILYN
How long?

CHRIS
45 minutes.

MARILYN
No problem.

CHRIS
Would you be able to work immediately?

MARILYN
It's short notice, but I could do it. What would I be modeling?

CHRIS
You'd be undraped.

MARILYN
So I'd be wearing a toga?

CHRIS
You'd be nude.

Marilyn gives Shay a WTF? look. Chris knows the look.

MARILYN
Oh no– NO!

All About Marilyn

SHAYLA
It's an art class. Ain't nobody thinking about your behind but you.

MARILYN
Says the sista pimping me out to academia—

CHRIS
Marilyn, let me assure you in there is nothing sexual or pornographic about nudity in a figure drawing class-

MARILYN
Tell that to the students.

CHRIS
My students are thinking about nothing but line, composition, and form. There are strict rules for conduct in a fine arts class. We have zero tolerance for sexual harassment.

Marilyn is reassured but a little nervous.

MARILYN
They can't touch me?

CHRIS
They can't even talk to you during the session. Before the class begins, you're in a dressing room connected to the classroom with its own separate entrance and exit. I'm the only person who will interact with you during class.

SHAYLA
Relax. This isn't Dark Ride.

MARILYN
I guess it won't be too bad. How much are you paying for the session?

CHRIS
Two hundred dollars. Cash.

MARILYN
When would you need me?

CHRIS
It's a noon class so if you could be here around eleven tomorrow that would be great.

MARILYN
I'll be here. Thanks.

Marilyn shakes Chris' hand. She and Shay walk out into the–

HALLWAY

MARILYN
Nice guy.

SHAYLA
He is. I'll show you where the gym is.

MARILYN
I have something to say to you Shay.

SHAYLA
What?

MARILYN
You stink.

Shay laughs.

SHAYLA
Why?

All About Marilyn

                    MARILYN
First day in the city and you got me posing nude for some dude. I feel like I'm back in L.A.

                    SHAYLA
Well, you have to put yourself out there if you want to get work.

Marilyn laughs as they leave the Fine Arts building. Across the street at the–

EXT. BODYWORKS – EVENING

People can be seen in the storefront display window walking on treadmills. Shay opens the door of–

INT. BODYWORKS – EVENING

A trendy New York health club. Hardbodies working out. Marilyn and Shayla walk up to the–

RECEPTION DESK

Where Shayla swipes her membership card.

                    SHAYLA
She's with me.

Marilyn is handed a guest pass. She sticks it on the breast of her polo across from the college guest pass. The women walk around the front desk. Marilyn gets a sense of the club and notices–

ERIC JAMES, 34, a handsome clean-cut brother in crinkle pants and a T-shirt headed towards the treadmills. Husky and somewhat awkward, he doesn't fit in with the rest of the hardbodies. Club regulars laugh as he starts walking the treadmill. It gets the better of him. Marilyn doesn't find it funny.

                    MARILYN
Seems like the regulars find him entertaining.

                    SHAYLA
He signed up last week. Bought the deluxe package.

                    MARILYN
He's not going to last long. He doesn't know his way around the equipment.

The RECEPTIONIST, 21, in bright spandex overhears the conversation. A gum popping Long Island type, she's ready to get into Marilyn's business.

                    RECEPTIONIST
You got that right honey. Four, five visits more and he's going to quit. Easiest money we ever made.

Marilyn keeps her eye on Eric and gets into the receptionist's business.

                    MARILYN
What kind of facilities do you have?

                    RECEPTIONIST
Well, there's an aerobic studio in the back, and the weight-training studio here in the front. We also have classes for tai chi, yoga, and Pilates upstairs.

                    MARILYN
And your locker rooms?

All About Marilyn

RECEPTIONIST
Down the hall. We have full showers and towels for members, along with a steam room and hot tubs. Would you like to speak to a sales rep?

MARILYN
Would it be possible for me to do a workout here on my friend's pass? I want to get a sense of the club and the equipment before I sign up for a membership.

The Receptionist is eager to get the sale.

RECEPTIONIST
Management frowns on it, but I could let you slide one time since you're thinking about buying a membership. Come in tomorrow around one or two.

MARILYN
Thanks.

Marilyn and Shayla leave the club. Shayla checks her watch–

SHAYLA
It's still early. I could drive you back uptown–

MARILYN
No I'll wait for you.

SHAYLA
You can hang out in my office then. After I teach this class I'll be done for today.

MARILYN
Oh no, I want to see the great Professor Shayla Sims in action!

SHAYLA
I have something to say to you Marilyn.

MARILYN
What?

SHAYLA
You stink.

The women laugh and walk around corner and enter a building with a blue flag draped outside stating LIBERAL ARTS AND SCIENCES that's–

INT. NEXT SCHOOL LIBERAL ARTS BLDG LOBBY – EVENING

Clean and quiet. Kids are sitting in the lounge and surfing the net on public computers. Marilyn and Shayla pass by security and head down the hall to-

ROOM 167

A small intimate classroom. Most of the students are already there. Marilyn takes a seat up front. She doesn't want to miss a minute of this. A student sitting next to her asks–

STUDENT
You a late entrant into the class?

Marilyn smiles at the compliment.

MARILYN
I'm just checking out the school.

Shayla gets the class started.

All About Marilyn

              SHAYLA
Okay class, we were talking about the role of African-Americans in media last time—

Marilyn is engrossed. 90 minutes later...

She's out like a light. Class is over, kids are walking out. The student sitting next to Marilyn is about to wake her— Shayla waves her off. She nudges Marilyn—

              MARILYN
Wha... Shay?

              SHAYLA
You fell asleep in my class.

              MARILYN
I'm sorry. I guess I was a bit jetlagged.

              SHAYLA
Yeah, well you've had a long day. I'll get you home so you can sleep it off.

Sleepy Marilyn staggers up and follows Shayla out of the building. Cool night air wakes her up before they get into—

INT. SHAYLA'S SUV – NIGHT

MOVING

And head uptown.

              SHAYLA
So what did you think of my teaching? The parts you stayed awake for?

              MARILYN
I really liked the way you teach. You get everyone involved in the lesson.

SHAYLA
Except for sleepy California girls.

MARILYN
It was the tryptophan in the airline turkey.

SHAYLA
Would you think about going to school here?

MARILYN
I may have to add the Next School to my list of possible candidates.

SHAYLA
Is it the close proximity to the gym or Mr. Awkward?

Marilyn is busted. She tries to play it off–

MARILYN
I was not checking him out!

SHAYLA
No, no, don't try to front. You had your eye on a brother–

MARILYN
Everyone had an eye on him–

SHAYLA
Come on, you have a right to look. I mean what has it been ten? Fifteen years since you last dated–

MARILYN
Look, this is a career related dry spell. You know how hard it is for me to get a date–

All About Marilyn

SHAYLA
Yes, the curse of being a beautiful celebrity. You've explained your "Bermuda Triangle" theory to me many, many times over the phone.

MARILYN
Every Saturday night after I actually washed my hair.

SHAYLA
Hey, I bought you the shampoo a couple of times.

MARILYN
Brothers get either get intimidated because they think I'm rich, or they get intimidated because they saw me on TV, or they get intimidated because they think I'm Nikki Desmond.

SHAYLA
If there was only a cure for male pattern insecurity.

MARILYN
Why didn't you help him out?

SHAYLA
Marilyn, I am married. I do not need Terrence coming down to that gym to beat that poor boy down in front of people.

MARILYN
Yeah, I can see how that could get awkward. How long has he been going down there?

SHAYLA
I knew you were checking him out!

                    MARILYN
            Okay, so I admit it. So how many workouts
            has he been there for?

                    SHAYLA
            Every other day. You planning on stepping to
            him?

                    MARILYN
            If he's there tomorrow and I'm there I might
            give him some workout tips.

Shayla drives over to–

EXT. LENOX TERRACE – NIGHT

A clean well-lit luxury building. Shayla parks in space 5A. She takes Marilyn's luggage out and they walk down the pathway. The Doorman lets them in and they walk into –

INT. LENOX TERRACE LOBBY – NIGHT

Decorated with Berber carpets and green plants. Marilyn presents her deed to Doorman. He has something for her–

                    DOORMAN
            Oh, these came for you Ms. Marie.

And rolls out a cart with boxes containing Marilyn's personal effects. Shay stuffs the bags on the top shelf.

                    MARILYN
                  (Tipping him)
            Thanks.

Marilyn rolls the cart into the–

All About Marilyn

ELEVATOR

And they get off on the—

FIFTH FLOOR

A narrow Berber carpeted corridor with a painting of the Apollo Theatre on the wall. Apartment #5A is right across the hall. Anticipation builds as Marilyn unlocks door to—

INT. MARILYN'S APARTMENT LIVING ROOM – NIGHT

A large, well-lit old style apartment decorated with expensive modern furniture, plush carpet, and brand new state of the art electronics. Shayla and Marilyn roll the cart next to the foyer closet and they look around.

                    MARILYN
    They went all out.

                    SHAYLA
    That's an understatement. This is way better
    than your old place! I could see myself
    hanging out here all the time—

Shay pauses when—

She finds the black and white portrait of Marilyn's stitched up face framed on the left wall. She's disturbed by what she sees in it.

                    SHAYLA
    Oh my God.

                    MARILYN
    It's right where I wanted it.

                    SHAYLA
    Why would you want that on your wall?

MARILYN
It's the most beautiful picture I've ever taken.

SHAYLA
But you're scarred–

MARILYN
Not on the inside.

Shayla studies the photo again and sees her best friend's inner beauty for the first time.

MARILYN
My TV and movie memorabilia is going to be displayed around it. It's going to tell the story of my career in pictures.

SHAYLA
You want some help setting this up?

Marilyn looks across at boxes then at her watch. It's a lot of work and she's had a long day.

MARILYN
(Yawning)
We'll probably get to it later next week. I really want to get some sleep.

SHAYLA
Okay. What time do you want me to pick you up tomorrow?

Marilyn and Shayla walk over to the apartment door.

MARILYN
I'll meet you outside the building at ten.

Marilyn lets Shayla out, locks up, and shuffles into her–

All About Marilyn

BEDROOM

Large and stylish, decorated with top of the line furniture. An LCD TV on the wall above the dresser. Marilyn peels out of her clothes–

And falls into bed. She's sprawled out on the comforter until the–

NEXT MORNING

Sunlight shines in the bedroom window. BEEP! BEEP! BEEP! BEEP! Marilyn's wristwatch alarm goes off. Nine A.M. Marilyn hurries into the–

LIVING ROOM

Where she grabs her suitcase and carry-on and heads into the–

BEDROOM

To empty the contents of her carry-on on the bed and open her suitcase. She lays out gym clothes, a silk robe, new Mary Jane sneakers, and her outfit for the day. Everything is black, a powerful contrast to baby blue comforter. Marilyn grabs her toiletries bag and hurries into the–

BATHROOM

Decorated with top of the line fixtures, a pedestal tub, and Turkish towels. Marilyn showers, towels off, and brushes her hair. She puts on deodorant, red lipstick and rushes–

BACK INTO THE BEDROOM

And quickly gets dressed in a black fitted blouse, pencil skirt and Mary Jane sneakers. She grabs her gym clothes and stuffs them in the carry-on bag along with her wallet and cell phone. She slings it over her shoulder–

And heads out of the apartment downstairs to the–

LOBBY

Where the Doorman lets her out. She gets in–

INT. SHAYLA'S SUV – MORNING

And rides shotgun as the truck is–

MOVING

Into light midday traffic on city streets.

                    MARILYN
     Morning Shay.

                    SHAYLA
     Morning Marilyn. How'd you sleep?

                    MARILYN
     Like a log.

Shayla reaches into inside her suit pocket and hands Marilyn her gym card.

                    SHAYLA
     Get this back to me tonight.

                    MARILYN
     I'm not going to lose it. Which locker is yours?

                    SHAYLA
     Mine is 537. The combination is 34 left, 30 right, and 9 left.

                    SHAYLA
     You nervous about today?

All About Marilyn

> **MARILYN**
> A little. You know how I am first day on a gig.

Shay drives downtown. She stops off in front of the—

FINE ARTS BUILDING

Where Marilyn grabs her bag and gets out. Shay tells her—

> **SHAYLA**
> Next week we start taking the subway like regular people.

> **MARILYN**
> Crowded in a metal box in a hole in the ground. Should be fun.

> **SHAYLA**
> Yeah, lots of fun as long as you don't make eye contact with anyone. I'll meet you outside the gym at seven.

Shayla drives around the corner. Marilyn walks into the—

INT. FINE ARTS BUILDING LOBBY – MORNING

Signs in, gets a guest pass, and heads down the hall to—

CHRIS' OFFICE

Chris is at his desk looking over a sketch. He lights up when Marilyn walks into the room.

> **CHRIS**
> Ah, Marilyn you're early.

> MARILYN
> I wanted to get a sense of the classroom, talk about what kind of poses you want me to get into.

> CHRIS
> (Checking watch)
> Well, it's almost time for class. We'll talk more in the studio.

Chris gets up. They walk down the hall and turn the corner to the front door of–

STUDIO 1A

Chris jiggles keys and unlocks–

STUDIO 1A

A big room with easels and stools set up in a circle. When Marilyn and Chris walk into the center of the room he gives her an earnest look.

> MARILYN
> Looks intimate.

> CHRIS
> There will only be twelve students in the class. You'll be standing here. The tape on the floor is your mark.

Marilyn looks down and sees the white tape X.

> MARILYN
> What kind of pose do you want me to be in?

All About Marilyn

CHRIS
It's a beginner class. Since it's your first time modeling with me, we're going to keep it basic. Just stand like you usually would.

MARILYN
Okay.

Chris leads Marilyn across room. He opens the door of the–

DRESSING ROOM

A small room with props scattered about. A full-length mirror on the exit door, a green light above the entrance door.

CHRIS
That door locks from the inside only. It leads to a hallway out to the lobby. About twenty minutes before the end of class I'll signal to you and you'll leave the room to get dressed. I'll meet you outside in the hall about ten minutes after.

MARILYN
You're really organized. I'm really not going to interact with anyone.

CHRIS
We keep it professional here in Fine Arts. It's school policy for all models to leave the building before the class is dismissed.

MARILYN
How will I know to come out?

Chris points up to green light above dressing room door. Marilyn looks up.

CHRIS

See that light up there? When it lights up you'll come out walk to the center of the room and disrobe.

MARILYN

Wow, this is just like acting. I've got cues and everything.

CHRIS

The art studio is like a stage. With good timing and execution we can make some quality pieces today.

CHRIS

I'll see you in a couple of minutes.

Chris leaves and closes the door. The sounds of students WALKING into the classroom and CHATTING can be heard outside. Marilyn opens the exit door–

And sees the hall. She knows she's safe. She locks the door and takes a deep breath as–

She drops her bag and steps out of her Mary Janes. A nervous Marilyn stares at her reflection as–

She unbuttons her blouse. It falls on top of the bag next to her followed by–

Her skirt, –

Her bra, –

And finally her panties. Nude–

All About Marilyn

Marilyn checks herself out in the mirror again. She's still a little tense, but she's confident she can do this. She takes a deep breath and relaxes after doing a few goofy poses in front of the mirror and making some silly faces. She hears Chris LECTURING the class on body language as–

She slips on her robe. The green light comes on and–

She strolls out of the dressing room–

BACK INTO THE STUDIO

Smiles, unties her robe, and makes eye contact with everyone. She feels the creative energy in the room as–

The robe falls on the stool behind her. Chris tells the students–

                CHRIS
    You have forty-five minutes to sketch your
    figure.

Kids sketch, Marilyn is glowing. Time breezes by. Chris gestures–

And Marilyn throws on her robe. She wishes she could stay longer, but heads back into the–

DRESSING ROOM

And gets changed back into street clothes. Her bag is slung over her shoulder and she's stepping into her shoes when she hears–

KNOCK! KNOCK! KNOCK! A rapp on the door. Marilyn opens the door to–

Greet Chris with a smile. He has two one hundred dollar bills in hand.

                CHRIS
    Thank you very much.

                    MARILYN
              (Stuffing money into wallet)
          Always glad to help Chris.

Marilyn strolls down hall smiling. She had more fun than she expected to. She leaves the Fine Arts Building and heads across street into the—

INT. BODYWORKS – AFTERNOON

Where the receptionist remembers her and waves her in. Marilyn heads into the—

LADIES LOCKER ROOM

A high-quality changing area, but not as luxurious as Jim's. Ceramic tiled floors, Turkish towels, and teak benches. Hardbodies undressed. Marilyn finds locker 537, works the combination, and—

POP! Shay's locker opens up. Marilyn changes into black spandex and hits the—

GYM FLOOR

Where the action on the floor is light, most machines are available. Marilyn starts her workout with a run on the treadmill. She sees—

ANGLE TO RECEPTION DESK

Eric coming in wearing a dress shirt, slacks, and a tie. The woman on the treadmill across from her laughs out loud in anticipation of another hilarious episode. Marilyn smiles, gets a good stride going as—

BACK ON THE GYM FLOOR

Eric hits the floor in sweats and T-shirt. He makes a bee-line for the bench press, sets it for 150. He lifts and strains as the—

All About Marilyn

Woman running on the treadmill next to Marilyn's busts a gut. Marilyn has seen enough. She slides off her treadmill, strolls over to the bench press and grabs the bars. Eric makes eye contact and catches Marilyn's smile. Her beauty stuns him.

> **MARILYN**
> Are you pressing the weights or are the weights pressing you?

> **ERIC**
> I was just trying to get something going.

> **MARILYN**
> The only thing you're going to get going is a hernia like this.

> **ERIC**
> So how would a brother like me get something going?

Marilyn is ready to share what she knows.

> **MARILYN**
> First you have to stretch. Get your muscles loose before you work on the equipment. That way you won't hurt yourself.

Marilyn takes Eric's hand to help him off the bench. She feels some sparks as they touch.

> **MARILYN**
> Let's go over here–

> **ERIC**
> Eric. Eric James.

> **MARILYN**
> Okay Eric let's go over to the treadmills. After that I'll show you how to use the equipment.

Marilyn walks Eric over to a treadmill. He gets on, she programs it. Eric builds a pace as Marilyn gets to know him.

> MARILYN
> This will get your muscles stretched out. Once you build up a good stride you'll be warmed up for work on the weight machines.

> ERIC
> In my old high school gym class we used to stretch–

> MARILYN
> This works better. How long have you been working out?

> ERIC
> I just started last week. I thought I'd get into shape. It's something I always wanted to do.

> MARILYN
> But you got picked on in gym class.

> ERIC
> How'd you know?

> MARILYN
> You weren't exactly an expert on the bench press.

> ERIC
> I thought the machines were just like the ones I used to use back in the day.

> MARILYN
> Well, a lot about fitness has changed since then.

Women walk by and laugh. Eric puts his head down.

All About Marilyn

ERIC
The people haven't.

Marilyn gets Eric's eyes back on her.

MARILYN
First rule in a gym: Don't let the regulars intimidate you.

ERIC
Because they're insecure?

MARILYN
No...because they're part of the scam.

ERIC
They're ripping me off–

MARILYN
No, your contract is legit. But the scheme with gyms is in the environment. The regulars intimidate newbies like you, get you discouraged, and then you quit after a couple of visits. You'll still have paid for a year of membership.

ERIC
I paid for two years–

MARILYN
I know. I heard them talking about how you bought the deluxe package at the front desk.

ERIC
You're not going to let me quit.

                    MARILYN
You obviously came here because you want to better yourself. I want to help you meet your fitness goals.

                    ERIC
Are you a trainer?

                    MARILYN
Nah. Just someone who wants to be your friend.

Eric smiles. He wants to be her friend too.

                    ERIC
I wouldn't mind having a friend like you.

                    MARILYN
Great. I'll show you how to bench right. Then we'll do a circuit.

Eric gives her a look as he slides off the treadmill.

                    ERIC
You're not going to kill me are you?

Marilyn smiles at him.

                    MARILYN
You're going to have a lot of fun.

Marilyn leads Eric over to the bench press. They do a circuit, working every machine on the floor. At the end of the session, both are sweaty and satisfied as they walk over to the–

RECEPTION DESK

Where Eric catches his breath. The receptionist is eager to hear some gossip.

All About Marilyn

RECEPTIONIST
So how did you like our club?

MARILYN
You have good equipment. I could see myself working out here all the time.

RECEPTIONIST
So can I sign you up?

MARILYN
Yeah.

The receptionist hands Marilyn an application. Marilyn takes it off the clipboard and tells her–

MARILYN
I'll get this back to you tomorrow.

RECEPTIONIST
(Frowning)
Okay.

The Receptionist sulks. Eric manages to compose himself. They walk over to the–

LOCKER ROOM ENTRANCE

ERIC
I thought you were going to join.

MARILYN
Second trick of the gym: Never fill out the application at the club. Too much pressure from salespeople. They get you to buy add-ons to packages you don't need.

ERIC
You seem to know a lot about the gym. How long have you been working out?

MARILYN
Oh, sixteen, seventeen years.

ERIC
No wonder you're so cut. You put a hurtin' on a brother.

Marilyn blushes. She pats on Eric stomach playfully then tells him–

MARILYN
You'll get used to it after a couple of weeks. Tone up all this nice soft stuff here.

ERIC
You want to get a juice or something? Er... Miss–

Marilyn is caught off guard. It's the first time she's been asked out in 15 years.

MARILYN
My friends call me Marilyn. And that would be great. Just let me shower and change. Meet me back here in a half-hour.

ERIC
Cool.

Both strut into their respective locker rooms. A half-hour later they return to the–

LOCKER ROOM ENTRANCE

And light up at the sight of each other in street clothes. They leave the Bodyworks and head out to–

All About Marilyn

EXT. 14th STREET SIDEWALK – EVENING

And walk around the corner into–

INT. REST OR RANT – EVENING

A stylish greasy spoon. They grab a booth and drop their bags. The waitress presents them with water and menus.

> ERIC
> I'll have an orange juice, a turkey burger, and fries.

> MARILYN
> I'll have a Coke, a turkey burger, and fries.

> ERIC
> Coke? I thought you wanted a juice–

> MARILYN
> You wanted a juice. I'm having a Coke.

> ERIC
> You are something else Marilyn.

The waitress walks away. Marilyn asks–

> MARILYN
> So what do you do for a living Mr. James?

> ERIC
> I'm in Marketing. I work right across the street from the club. What do you do?

The waitress brings their meals over. They chow down.

> MARILYN
> I'm getting ready to go to school right now.

ERIC
I thought you were a trainer. The way you know your way around a gym–

MARILYN
Working out was part of my old job. You had to keep your body tight in my old line of work.

ERIC
What did you used to do?

MARILYN
Oh, I used to work in TV out in Burbank.

ERIC
So you worked on a TV show?

MARILYN
Somewhat. I did everything wanted to do out there so I came to the city for a fresh start.

ERIC
I could understand that. Sometimes it's best to move on than stay in a job that goes nowhere.

MARILYN
I'm looking to have some fun. Are you a lot of fun Eric?

ERIC
I'd like to think I'm interesting.

MARILYN
I think you are. So how many times a week do you work out?

All About Marilyn

ERIC
Every other day. Most times I put in a workout after work around five or so.

MARILYN
It's a good schedule. It gives the muscles time to rest.

ERIC
You have a plan for me?

MARILYN
You work with me and I'll work with you.

ERIC
When can we meet again— for another workout?

Marilyn checks her watch. Six-fifty-eight already.

MARILYN
Er…do you have a card?

Eric reaches into pocket for a business card. The waitress presents the check.

ERIC
The red number is my office. The black is my cell.

MARILYN
I'll give you a call tomorrow and we'll set up a schedule.

Marilyn stuffs Eric's card into her pocket.

ERIC
Cool. I'll walk you out.

Eric pays the bill and they leave. They walk around the corner to–

EXT. BODYWORKS – NIGHT

Where Shayla is waiting in her SUV. Marilyn waves goodbye to Eric and gets in–

INT. SHAYLA'S SUV – NIGHT

MOVING

And hands Shay her gym membership card. Shay is ready to hear the dish as they drive off.

                SHAYLA
Were you working on your body or your game?

                MARILYN
A little of both. His name is Eric and he works around the corner.

                SHAYLA
What's he like?

                MARILYN
He's nice. I could see us hanging out.

                SHAYLA
He get those digits?

                MARILYN
I have his card. I'll give him a call tomorrow. We're going to discuss a workout schedule for him.

                SHAYLA
You're moving fast.

All About Marilyn

MARILYN
When I see an opportunity I go for it.

SHAYLA
So how'd the modeling job go?

MARILYN
Better than I thought. I actually had fun.

SHAYLA
You think you'd do it again?

MARILYN
I would. With all the cues and stuff it's just like acting.

SHAYLA
So you didn't mind the nudity?

MARILYN
I was so in the zone I forgot I was nude.

SHAYLA
Are you going out tomorrow?

MARILYN
You have someplace to be?

SHAYLA
I have four classes and I have to pick up Thomas from Daycare after work. So if you need to go somewhere–

MARILYN
It's okay. I might just walk around the neighborhood, pick up some groceries, and sleep in. I mean, two days in New York and I've already met a guy and worked a gig.

                SHAYLA
Yeah, that's more than you did in five years in L.A.

                MARILYN
I should have moved here a long time ago.

Shayla drives to Marilyn's building drops her off in front of–

EXT. LENOX TERRACE – NIGHT

Marilyn waves as Shayla drives off. The Doorman lets her in and she heads upstairs to–

INT. MARILYN'S APARTMENT LIVING ROOM – NIGHT

Her apartment. She kicks off her shoes, drops her bag, and flops on the sofa when–

BRIIIING! Her cell phone rings. Marilyn unzips her bag and picks it up–

                MARILYN
Marilyn Marie.

                CHRIS
                (On phone)
Marilyn, this is Chris from the Next School. I was reviewing the sketches from our session and I wanted to discuss the work with you. Could you come down to my office tomorrow?

                MARILYN
Sure. What time would you want me to come by?

All About Marilyn

CHRIS
(On phone)
I have some free time around noon.

MARILYN
Noon would be fine—

It hits Marilyn in the head that Shayla can't drive her. She needs a new plan.

MARILYN
Oh, I'm kind of new to the city, so what train would I take to get to the college?

CHRIS
(On phone)
Where are you staying?

MARILYN
135th and Lenox.

CHRIS
(On phone)
The 2 or 3 train will put you off right around the corner from the school. The subway station should be right around your building.

MARILYN
Thanks. See you tomorrow.

Marilyn hangs up, opens her bag, and pulls out a subway map and the membership application. She studies the red line of the IRT 7th Avenue line and smiles as the—

NEXT DAY

She rides in a crowded—

INT. IRT SUBWAY CAR – AFTERNOON

Number 3 express train. Marilyn dressed in a black business skirt, ballet flats, and a white blouse stands in the middle of throngs of passengers carrying her portfolio. The train bolts into–

INT. 14th STREET STATION – AFTERNOON

A busy express stop. Marilyn gets off the train, heads through the turnstile and up the stairs where–

EXT. 14th AND SEVENTH – AFTERNOON

The neighborhood looks familiar. Marilyn checks her watch–

She has time to spare. She makes it around the corner and heads into the-

INT. FINE ARTS BUILDING – AFTERNOON

Signs in, sticks on a guest pass, and makes a bee-line for–

CHRIS' OFFICE

Where he's reviewing sketches. He lights up when Marilyn walks in.

                CHRIS
Marilyn I'm glad you came. Have a seat.

              MARILYN
What's up?

                CHRIS
As I stated last night, I was reviewing the sketches and the work was very inspired. I especially love how they captured your face.

All About Marilyn

Chris hands her the sketches. The artwork is detailed, dynamic, and full of energy. Marilyn's spirit is captured in the face of the drawings.

MARILYN
It seems like they got my best side.

CHRIS
Usually my beginner classes don't draw this well. These are almost the level of an advanced level student.

MARILYN
What would your students have to do with me?

CHRIS
There was something, an energy during the session I felt coming from you. The class did too.

MARILYN
I was just being myself.

CHRIS
Have you found a job yet?

MARILYN
I've only been in the city two days.

CHRIS
I'd love to work with you again. In fact, I'd like to hire you as our model for the remainder of the semester. You have good lines, excellent muscle tone, no tattoos–

MARILYN
Are you coming on to me?

CHRIS
I have a wife, three kids and tenure at a job I love. You're not pretty enough for me to mess that up.

Marilyn stings from the ego punch. Ouch!

MARILYN
I'm just saying at two hundred dollars a session it could get a little costly.

CHRIS
Any price would be well worth it to get work like this out of my students. In addition to the model work, I wanted to make you aware of a Teacher's Assistant position here at the school next semester.

Marilyn doesn't know what to say.

MARILYN
I–I'm just an actress. I don't know how to file or type–

CHRIS
Then learn how to.

MARILYN
I doubt you'd have the patience to put up with me–

CHRIS
Marilyn, this is a college. No one came here knowing how to do anything, even me. The only reason people are here is to learn.

MARILYN
You pose a very unique argument.

All About Marilyn

CHRIS
I always try to teach my students to think outside of the box. Did you know my staff ID card allows me access to the entire campus?

MARILYN
And mine would hypothetically–

CHRIS
Allow you to use our libraries, computer labs, and archives. You'd also get discounts at bookstores, museums, and movie theatres.

MARILYN
Wow. Those are a lot of perks.

CHRIS
That's only the tip of the iceberg. Staff here also get free medical, dental, and a pension in addition to free tuition and books for their coursework.

MARILYN
You've been talking to Shay–

CHRIS
I merely wanted to make you aware of all the opportunities our school would offer. Over the course of four years you'd be saving over $150,000. Even more if you pursue a Master's or a Doctorate.

MARILYN
That's a lot of money for standing around naked in a classroom–

Chris lets the cat out of the bag.

CHRIS
Much, much more than your settlement with Apex Studios.

MARILYN
I knew you were talking to Shay!

CHRIS
No, I just know how these settlements are broken down. By the time all the legal fees, taxes, and other court costs are broken down there's very little money left for the plaintiff.

MARILYN
I thought you were an art professor–

CHRIS
My wife is an attorney. I don't want to see you end up where you were in L.A.

MARILYN
Wow. I didn't even see where I was going–

CHRIS
That's because you don't think outside of the box.

MARILYN
So how would you teach me to think outside of the box?

CHRIS
I take it you're accepting my offer.

MARILYN
I'd be a fool to pass it up.

Marilyn and Chris shake hands–

All About Marilyn

                    CHRIS
        Let's take care of your paperwork.

Marilyn and Chris work on employment paperwork, then head down to the hall into the–

PERSONNEL OFFICE

Where FLASH! There's a movie star smile on her new Next School I.D. card. It's clipped to her blouse as she and Chris head into the–

ADMISSIONS OFFICE

Where Marilyn walks out with an application packet. She waves goodbye to Chris after leaving the building and heads across the street into the–

INT. BODYWORKS – AFTERNOON

Where the Receptionist smiles when she sees her. She kept her word!

                    MARILYN
        I'd like to sign up for a membership.

Ten minutes later Marilyn walks out of the club–

EXT. 14th STREET – AFTERNOON

Tucking a Bodyworks membership card in her shirt pocket. She eases her cell phone and Eric's business card out of her skirt pocket, punches in the number and– BRRING! The phone rings–

                    ERIC
                  (On phone)
        Eric James.

MARILYN
Hey Eric, it's Marilyn. What are you doing for lunch?

ERIC
(On phone)
I was working through lunch–

MARILYN
On a nice day like this? C'mon you have to go out on a day like this.

ERIC
(On phone)
Are you downstairs?

MARILYN
I'll meet you outside of the Bodyworks in ten minutes.

Marilyn waits as–

Eric in shirt, tie, and slacks strolls around the corner. He lights up at the sight of her. She's happy to see him too.

ERIC
Hey Marilyn what's up?

MARILYN
I was in the neighborhood. Just wanted to touch base with you.

ERIC
What type of workout are we doing today? I didn't bring my gear with me–

MARILYN
You don't need your gear to exercise. We can just walk around.

All About Marilyn

ERIC
Is that what they do in California?

MARILYN
When we want to have fun.

ERIC
I know a place we can hang out.

Eric and Marilyn walk up 14th Street cross-town. A curious Marilyn inquires–

MARILYN
So where are we going?

ERIC
Union Square. It's a nice place to sit on days like this.

MARILYN
You go there all the time?

ERIC
Sometimes. What brought you by my part of town?

MARILYN
I wanted to see about a job at the school.

ERIC
How'd it go?

MARILYN
I start Monday.

ERIC
That's great!

MARILYN
Yeah, I'm getting ready to get enrolled and stuff.

ERIC
What are you going to be majoring in?

MARILYN
I'm taking mostly introductory stuff this year.

ERIC
You're so good with training I thought you'd major in physical therapy.

MARILYN
Even if I did training as a career, I'd need to learn how to do my books. So it's best to keep my options open.

Eric smiles when Marilyn's eyes light up upon seeing the trees on the promenade of—

UNION SQUARE PARK

A busy farmer's market full of vendors, customers, and tourists. Marilyn smiles and takes Eric's hand as they find an intimate spot on a—

PARK BENCH

ERIC
So, what are your plans for us working out?

MARILYN
Like I said yesterday, you work with me and I'll work with you.

ERIC
Is this part of your plan?

All About Marilyn

MARILYN
Well, exercise is something you can do anywhere at any time. The main goal is having fun.

ERIC
Like we're having now.

MARILYN
Now you're getting it.

ERIC
So… Marilyn are you seeing someone?

MARILYN
Nah. I just got in the city a couple of days ago.

Eric smiles. He has a shot.

ERIC
No wonder you're used to this heat. Everybody else would want to stay in with the air conditioning.

MARILYN
Is that how you New Yorkers deal with Summer?

ERIC
Yeah.

MARILYN
So are you seeing anyone Mr. James?

ERIC
Nah.

Eric steps up his game.

ERIC
So what are you going to be doing at the college at your job?

MARILYN
I'm going to be a model in the Art Dept. Do some administrative work in the office too. You want to see some sketches the kids drew of me?

Marilyn hands Eric the sketches. Marilyn laughs out loud catching his awkward reaction. Eric tries to play it off.

ERIC
These are nice. I love the way they captured your face.

MARILYN
Thanks.

ERIC
You do know you are nude in these.

MARILYN
I thought you were looking at my face–

ERIC
I was looking at your face. Now I have a visual of what's under the spandex.

MARILYN
You're not going to have a problem with me doing this kind of work are you?

ERIC
Everybody has to make a living.

All About Marilyn

> MARILYN
> Y'know you are really understanding about this. Most guys would pitch a fit.

> ERIC
> Nothing to pitch a fit about. Ain't nobody trying to lose their tenured good paying job over you.

> MARILYN
> That's what they tell me.

Eric leans back on the bench. He makes eye contact with Marilyn then glances at big clock on a building and realizes–

> ERIC
> Man, I've got to get back to the office. I'm expecting a call from a client.

> MARILYN
> Yeah, I have to go grocery shopping myself.

> ERIC
> I'll walk you back to the train station.

Marilyn and Eric hop off the bench and walk back cross-town. Eric waves at Marilyn as she heads into the train station. Forty-five minutes later…

EXT. 135th STREET SUBWAY ENTRANCE – AFTERNOON

She marches up the stairs of the 135th Street Station. Familiar surroundings. She heads into a nearby supermarket–

And comes out with grocery bags. She heads back home where she's–

INT. MARILYN'S APARTMENT KITCHEN – EVENING

Putting stuff in the fridge when–

BRRRING! Her cell phone rings. Marilyn takes the cell phone out of her pocket–

                MARILYN

Marilyn Marie.

                SABRINA
                (On phone)

Marilyn, this is Sabrina. They found your car. Only the frame was left.

                MARILYN

A year on the streets of L.A. we're lucky they even found a VIN number.

                SABRINA
                (On phone)

Lucky for you, the insurance company is paying off on it. I'll be sending you the check tomorrow.

                MARILYN

Thanks. Any luck with the Tower Board?

                SABRINA
                (On phone)

They're still dragging their feet. I think we may have to sue them.

                MARILYN

Do what you can Bri. I know how difficult Lori can be.

All About Marilyn

SABRINA
(On phone)
I just hope you find a way to pay your bills until you find a job.

MARILYN
Well, I won't have to worry about money too much. I just came back from an interview. I got a job at Shay's college.

SABRINA
(On phone)
That's great! Where are you working?

MARILYN
The Fine Art Department. I'm doing some modeling for now–

SABRINA
(On phone)
I thought you were leaving the business–

MARILYN
It's just some figure modeling until the next semester starts. Then I'll do some admin work in the professor's office.

SABRINA
(On phone)
I thought you weren't doing any more nudity after that whole Dark Ride fiasco–

MARILYN
Professor Cherry's class is way more professional than any movie set I've been on.

SABRINA
(On phone)
I take it you're adjusting to life in the city?

MARILYN
It's a faster vibe than L.A., but I'm getting used to it. I just rode the subway for the first time.

SABRINA
(On phone)
I hear you were also pursuing the opposite sex.

An embarrassed Marilyn blushes–

MARILYN
I'm gonna get Shay–

SABRINA
(On phone)
She's just looking out for you.

MARILYN
Okay, I met a guy at the gym. I'm helping him learn the machines.

SABRINA
(On phone)
Maybe you'll give him a workout in the bedroom–

MARILYN
BRI–!

SABRINA
(On phone)
Hey, I told you to go out and have some fun. My God, what's it been fifteen years? Get out there before your girl parts dry up.

MARILYN
You know about the Bermuda Triangle–

All About Marilyn

              SABRINA
              (On phone)
If you could move past Nikki Desmond, you can escape the Bermuda Triangle once and for all.

              MARILYN
Maybe it's possible. Talk to you later Bri.

Marilyn hits end, grabs the sketches, and heads into the–

LIVING ROOM

And walks over to the portrait of her scarred face. She flips though the pictures, finds one she likes and pins it on the right side of the portrait. She studies the sketch and–

Walks over to the boxes with her All About Nikki memorabilia and personal effects. She sets up the display on the left side of the portrait. Photos, posters, and memorabilia come together to tell her life story in pictures. There's lots of open space on the wall next to the sketch.

Marilyn sets up her tapes and TV props in the bookcase below. The last item she puts on display is a crystal clear bowling ball. The base she places it on says: "FROM EPISODE #2.08– "HAVE A BOWL". Marilyn smiles, looks down at ball, and gets ideas for…

DISSOLVE TO:

INT. BODYWORKS GYM FLOOR – AFTERNOON

Marilyn spots Eric on the bench. He's pressing 100, feeling the burn–

              MARILYN
Just one more rep. Just one more…

Eric pushes himself. Gets the bar up then rests it down. He eases up off the bench to Marilyn's delight.

> ERIC
> Whoa. Am I still alive?

> MARILYN
> (Checking Eric's pulse)
> Yep. You're still breathing.

> ERIC
> And you do this every day?

> MARILYN
> Yep. It's going to get easier once you get used to it.

> ERIC
> (Patting Marilyn's stomach)
> Maybe in a couple of months I can tone up all my soft stuff to be firm like yours.

Marilyn is feeling him.

> MARILYN
> (Poking Eric's stomach)
> I might want to keep this a little soft.

> ERIC
> So what are you doing Saturday?

> MARILYN
> Oh, I was going to ask you the same thing. Are there any bowling places around here?

> ERIC
> There's this place in Chelsea. You want to go?

All About Marilyn

> MARILYN
> I don't know my way around that well.

> ERIC
> I forgot you just got here. What train station do you live by?

> MARILYN
> 135th and Lenox.

> ERIC
> I'll meet you on the uptown side of the station around noon.

Marilyn struts to the showers feeling Eric's eyes on her. She smiles.

INT. MARILYN'S APARTMENT – AFTERNOON

Marilyn dressed in a black bowling shirt with Nikki's name embroidered on it and new black jeans grabs the crystal clear bowling ball off the top of the bookcase and stuffs it in her bowling bag. She heads out of the apartment, the building, and around the corner into–

INT. 135th STREET SUBWAY STATION – AFTERNOON

A remodeled subway station in gentrified Harlem. Marilyn hurries down the stairs through turnstile to meet–

Eric waiting for her on the platform dressed in jeans, oxford shirt, and Timberland spice tans. They light up on seeing each other.

> ERIC
> Nice shirt. Who's Nikki?

Marilyn plays it off.

> MARILYN
> I don't know, I got it at a thrift store.

ERIC
Have you bowled before?

MARILYN
A couple of times.

ERIC
I don't know a thing about this sport.

MARILYN
We've got to get you out more–

Marilyn is interrupted as–

The 2 train bolts into the station. They get on, get seats, and–

INT. IRT 2 TRAIN – AFTERNOON

MOVING

Marilyn gets to know Eric better as the train pulls out of the station.

MARILYN
So, Eric how long have you lived in New York?

ERIC
Born and raised here.

MARILYN
And you don't go anywhere?

ERIC
I never had a place to go. I'm so tired from working all week all I want to do is sleep on the weekend.

MARILYN
But you got up for me.

All About Marilyn

                    ERIC
         I wanted to have some fun.

Marilyn smiles as the train bolts into the—

23rd STREET STATION

A bustling local stop in Chelsea. Through the turnstile and up the stairs they head over to—

EXT. 300 NEW YORK BOWLING – AFTERNOON

A trendy Manhattan bowling alley at Chelsea Piers. They head over to the—

INT. FRONT COUNTER – AFTERNOON

Get some bowling shoes and hit—

LANE 8

Marilyn unzips the bag and reveals her crystal ball. Eric is surprised.

                    ERIC
         A clear bowling ball? I've never seen one of
         those before.

                    MARILYN
         It's my crystal ball.

                    ERIC
         What does it predict?

                    MARILYN
         (Waving hands over ball making gypsy voice)
         A victory on the lanes for me. For you a very,
         very bad beating.

Eric laughs as Marilyn hurls crystal ball down the lane…STRIKE! All the pins come crashing down until…

Hours later she scores a 269 Eric a 60. Eric pretends to feel bad about being whupped by a woman.

ERIC
Man, I can't believe I got whupped.

Marilyn smiles and pats Eric on the back.

MARILYN
Hey, 60 isn't bad for a beginner. You can only go up from here.

ERIC
I'm a represent next time.

MARILYN
(Putting her ball back in the bag)
The crystal ball sees it in your future.

Marilyn and Eric head out of the bowling alley back to the train station. A half hour later they're–

EXT. 135th STREET STATION ENTRANCE – AFTERNOON

Walking up the train station stairs laughing and joking. They turn the corner arriving at–

EXT. LENOX TERRACE LOBBY – AFTERNOON

Where they say their goodbyes. Inside–

INT. LENOX TERRACE LOBBY – AFTERNOON

Shayla sits in the lounge. She smiles watching them hold hands.

All About Marilyn

      MARILYN
I had a great time today.

      ERIC
I did too. We have to do this again.

      MARILYN
We definitely have to.

Marilyn and Eric are awkward. She goes for a kiss; Eric feels the vibe. He expects it on the lips. She's going that way, but–

Turns and pecks him the cheek. He knows she wanted to give it to him on the lips.

      MARILYN
I'll call you tonight.

      ERIC
Cool.

Eric heads home as Marilyn strolls into her building. Shay is eager to find out what's going on between them. She runs up to Marilyn ready to hear the dish as they get on the–

ELEVATOR

And head upstairs.

      SHAYLA
I thought you were staying in this weekend.

      MARILYN
Something came up. How long were you waiting for me?

      SHAYLA
I just got here. How'd your date go?

MARILYN
I had a blast. Eric is so much fun to hang out with.

SHAYLA
Hold on. How did the two of you go from workout partners to dating?

MARILYN
I was feeling him so I decided to go for it.

SHAYLA
You're moving kind of fast.

MARILYN
Hey, it was just bowling. I'm not bringing him up here to go to bed with me.

The elevator stops and opens on the—

FIFTH FLOOR

Marilyn gets out her keys and opens up—

INT. MARILYN'S APARTMENT – LIVING ROOM

Marilyn returns the crystal ball to its place in the display. Shay walks over—

SHAYLA
Oh, you got it up. I was going to help you with it today—

MARILYN
I was able to get things done on my own.

SHAYLA
Yeah I heard you also rode the subway for the first time—

All About Marilyn

MARILYN
Have you and Bri been talking about me again—

SHAYLA
No, Chris told me about you coming down for the interview. Congrats on the new job.

MARILYN
Thanks. I'm beginning to think my private life here is more public than my old Hollywood life—

SHAYLA
We all care about you Marilyn. We just want to make sure you're okay. I mean, you've been through a lot this past year.

MARILYN
I know.

SHAYLA
It's great you're doing stuff for yourself. It means we won't have to worry about you so much.

MARILYN
And you save a ton of money on gas.

SHAYLA
We were taking the subway next week—

MARILYN
And now you won't have to worry about me getting lost on Thursdays.

SHAYLA
No, you'll be at the gym working me over at lunchtime.

MARILYN
A small price to pay for a *foine* body. So what do you think?

SHAYLA
I thought you were just going to chronicle your career.

MARILYN
I thought I'd tell my life story in pictures instead.

SHAYLA
And the sketch?

MARILYN
It's supposed to represent my future. A rough unfinished work.

SHAYLA
I guess that's why you left all the other space on the side.

MARILYN
Yeah. I want to add more pictures–

SHAYLA
Of you and Eric?

Marilyn somberly looks at her reflection in the glass of the portrait frame.

MARILYN
I'm going to have to tell him.

SHAYLA
Tell him what?

All About Marilyn

MARILYN
(Gesturing to the All About Nikki poster)
About this.

SHAYLA
That's not who you are anymore. You don't have to say anything—

MARILYN
If I want a shot at a relationship with Eric he has to know all about Marilyn, not just the parts I feel comfortable with.

SHAYLA
You're entering the Bermuda Triangle again—

MARILYN
I'd rather he find out about it from me now than have it sprung on him later.

SHAYLA
Nikki Desmond is dead—

MARILYN
If I don't tell him her ghost will continue to haunt me.

SHAYLA
I hope you can escape the triangle this time.

Shay leaves. Marilyn flops on the sofa, turns on the TV, opens her cell phone, and punches in Eric's number. BRRRING! The phone rings—

ERIC
(On phone)
Eric James.

MARILYN
Hey Eric, it's Marilyn.

ERIC
(On phone)
Marilyn! What's up?

MARILYN
I was wondering if you could come by tomorrow morning. It's really important.

ERIC
(On phone)
I'll be there right after church.

Marilyn hits end. She flips channels until the—

NEXT MORNING

A tense Marilyn in a black silk robe and pajamas continues to flip through channels. She comes up on the news—

INSERT

NEWSCAST ON TV SCREEN

REPORTER
(On TV Screen)
Movie star Tabatha Strong and her bodyguard Jorge Ramos were arrested last night during a routine traffic stop on the Santa Monica Freeway. The 22-year-old star of the upcoming blockbuster SELL OUT was charged with possession of a controlled substance and assault on a police officer. Police allege packets of crystal meth and several pipes were found inside the SUV she was riding in.

All About Marilyn

Footage of Tabatha shown being dragged off in shackles by LAPD is followed by a mug shot of a dirty washed out junkie.

BACK TO THE LIVING ROOM

Marilyn into the story as–

BRRING! Her cell phone rings. She picks it up–

> SABRINA
> (On phone)
> Marilyn, did you hear about Tabatha?

> MARILYN
> I'm watching it now. No way she can get Hiram and his boys to bury this.

> SABRINA
> (On phone)
> They'll find a way to spin their way out of it. Probably get Tabatha another big money movie deal out of it.

> MARILYN
> Ah, the wacky world of Hollywood. I don't miss it for a minute. I just hope this doesn't hurt Garrett's box-office.

> SABRINA
> (On phone)
> More people will probably flock to the movie now because of all the bad press.

BZZZT! The intercom rings.

> MARILYN
> Bri, I have someone at the door. I'll talk to you later.

SABRINA
(On phone)
Yeah, I need to get some sleep. I didn't realize how early it was.

Marilyn hits end and heads over to the intercom phone on the wall.

DOORMAN
(On Intercom)
Ms. Marie, Eric James to see you.

MARILYN
Send him up.

Marilyn shuffles towards the door. She opens it–

And Eric in strolls in. She hugs him and gives him a kiss on the cheek to his surprise.

ERIC
Well, Good Morning to you too.

Marilyn closes the door behind him. She's scared to death. Eric catches the worried expression on her face–

ERIC
Is something wrong?

MARILYN
Yeah. Have a seat.

Eric takes a seat on the sofa. Marilyn changes the channel to an input screen, sits next to him, and takes his hand. She keeps her eyes on him; he spots the crystal ball but listens to her.

MARILYN
I wanted to talk to you about yesterday. When I kissed you–

All About Marilyn

ERIC
Did I do something wrong?

MARILYN
No. You were great. It's just— I have something to tell you.

MARILYN
Remember how I told you I worked in Burbank? How I worked in TV?

ERIC
Yeah—

MARILYN
Well, I didn't just work in TV. I was on TV.

ERIC
You're an actress.

MARILYN
Do you remember a show called All About Nikki?

ERIC
Yeah, I used to watch it all the time when I was in college. Man, she did some crazy stuff—

MARILYN
Yeah, it was a fun show.

Marilyn slinks up and grabs a videotape out of the display. Eric notices the pictures. He walks over—

ERIC
You must be a big fan of the show. You even have the dolls—

MARILYN
Yeah, I'm the ultimate Nikki Desmond fan.

ERIC
I knew that crystal ball was familiar–

MARILYN
A prop from one of the episodes. Nikki Desmond was so rich–

ERIC
She had a crystal bowling ball. Yeah, I remember that episode. She was trying to get this poor guy to like her so she pretended to–

Marilyn slips the tape in the VCR. The theme song plays. Eric looks up as the credits roll–

MARILYN
Do you know the name of the actress?

ERIC
I think her name was Marilyn–

MARILYN
My last name is Marie.

Eric looks at the All About Nikki poster, then Marilyn's name under the credits onscreen. He recognizes the faded teen star. He follows her pictures to the portrait of the disfigured Marilyn–

ERIC
What happened to you?

MARILYN
(Grabbing his hand)
I just want you to know I like you. I really like you. You're a nice guy–

All About Marilyn

ERIC
What happened to you?

MARILYN
Things didn't go in my career like I planned. A movie that was supposed to launch my film career flopped, I got typecast as Nikki Desmond, work was harder to get–

ERIC
What happened to your face?

MARILYN
I kept trying to get work, getting bit parts here and there, and taking handouts from friends to pay bills, working comicons–

ERIC
No, what happened to your face Marilyn?

Marilyn's eyes fall to the floor as she weeps.

MARILYN
I was on the set of a movie looking for work a year ago. Tabatha Strong saw me signing autographs for some kids. She attacked me with a bottle and cut up my face–

Marilyn lets it all out. A year of it. Eric holds her tightly. She breaks away. She can't stand to look at him.

MARILYN
The studio paid me to go away. They gave me a new face, some money and sent me here so Tabatha's public reputation wouldn't be ruined.

ERIC
They sacrificed you.

                    MARILYN
I just wanted you to know the truth about me.

                     ERIC
That's why you wouldn't kiss me on the lips.

                    MARILYN
It was a mistake.

                     ERIC
What we had yesterday wasn't a mistake–

                    MARILYN
No, this was a mistake. It wasn't right for me to bring you into my life. You wouldn't know how to deal with this. Hell, I don't know how to deal with this.

                     ERIC
You seemed to being doing a good job of dealing until now.

Marilyn walks Eric to the door and opens it.

                    MARILYN
I'm really sorry.

Eric walks out. Marilyn closes the door, runs over to the sofa and weeps bitterly as the All About Nikki episode onscreen fades to commercial–

DISSOLVE TO:

INT. BODYWORKS GYM FLOOR – AFTERNOON

Marilyn spots Shayla on the bench press. Shay is in the zone. Marilyn isn't feeling it today.

All About Marilyn

SHAYLA
I guess Eric is another man lost in the Bermuda Triangle.

MARILYN
I didn't want him to get near the water. I liked him too much.

SHAYLA
I still think you should have let him make the decision–

MARILYN
Nikki made the decision.

Eric dressed in sweats walks behind Marilyn–

ERIC
What does Marilyn have to say about us?

A startled Marilyn turns around. Shayla lights up.

SHAYLA
I'll be over by the treadmills.

Shayla excuses herself. Eric looks into Marilyn's eyes. She's afraid.

MARILYN
I thought I told you how I felt yesterday–

ERIC
I'm not giving up on you.

MARILYN
You know why we can't be close–

ERIC
Because you're scared.

MARILYN
You know the truth about me–

ERIC
That you're scared of me getting close to you.

MARILYN
Nikki and I are a package deal–

ERIC
Marilyn Marie is funnier, smarter, and more beautiful than any character she ever played on TV. I want to get to know her better.

MARILYN
You don't know what you're getting yourself into–

ERIC
It's obvious you came to New York because you wanted to better yourself. I want to help you achieve your personal goals.

MARILYN
My own words come back to haunt me.

ERIC
Man, I haven't seen an All About Nikki episode in ten years. I didn't know you played her until you put that tape on.

MARILYN
So you don't care about Nikki?

ERIC
I only care about Marilyn. Give me a chance to know all about you.

She looks into his eyes. She sees how much he cares and…

All About Marilyn

SMOOCH! She pecks Eric on the lips. She holds him close.

> MARILYN
> You're sweet.

> ERIC
> I guess that's from Saturday.

> MARILYN
> That's for believing in me.

> ERIC
> Stars come and go, but lights are hard to come by. I couldn't let you go out like that.

Marilyn remembers what Lucy told her.

> MARILYN
> Nice to know I inspired you.

> ERIC
> So are you going to give me a chance?

Marilyn answers his question with a kiss. They break the embrace and look into each other's eyes–

> MARILYN
> I want you to know all about me.

Marilyn walks Eric over to treadmills and introduces him to Shayla–

FADE OUT:

THE END.

Behind The Scenes

1990's teen sitcoms and the actors who starred in them.

No, it's not the topic of a daytime talk show. It's what inspired me to write this story.

Back in the late 1980's–early 1990's when I was a teenager/young adult I spent many a Saturday Morning or a weekday afternoon watching teen sitcoms. Shows like *Saved By The Bell*, *Charles In Charge*, *California Dreams*, *Student Bodies*, *City Guys*, *Sweet Valley High* and *Hang Time*. During the evenings, I watched prime-time stuff like *Fresh Prince of Bel-Air*, *Family Matters*, *Boy Meets World*, *Sister, Sister*, *Step by Step* and *Blossom*. I knew they were cheesy and were in no way a reflection of real life. But they were something to watch while doing homework or waiting for a more important program like wrestling to come on.

I never paid too much attention to the credits of those shows back then, but during a syndicated run of them from 2001–2004, I started to take a closer look at the credits putting names with faces. An Internet search of imdb.com, Wikipedia and thenandnow.net provided me with some surprising information on these actors.

I learned most of these low-budget sitcoms were huge moneymakers for the producers, cable networks, and the broadcast syndicators, but didn't pay much to the performers who starred in them. For some actors and actresses it was their first real acting job, a stepping-stone to higher paying work in prime-time shows and feature films. For others it was the first and last TV project they'd ever work in. Then there were the actors and actresses who struggled for years to find work doing guest spots in sitcoms, bit roles in made for-TV-movies and the occasional starring role in a direct-to-video movie. Working actors. Interesting people with a million untold stories. I felt a writing project coming on.

The story of a faded 1990's teen star excited me. She was like and old high school friend; I was eager to find out how she turned out years later. Did she become a superstar? Did she move on from her fifteen minutes of fame? Or was she crushed by years of rejection and forced into obscurity. There were so many questions I wanted to answer regarding her future. Unfortunately I was busy writing three other projects.

I sat on this story for three years and it's a good thing I did. All I really had was the premise: A typecast 1990's teen sitcom star reinvents herself in the 21st Century. The details were sketchy; her new identity was going to be something so campy and so ridiculous no one would think to look back at her acting past except the typical sitcom nosy neighbor. She was to talk in the third person and have a cheesy foreign accent. The whole thing was a bad idea right out of a teen sitcom except for the actress' real name: Marilyn Marie.

Marilyn Marie sounded like a movie star, close enough to Marilyn Monroe to be recognizable, but easily forgotten when compared to the iconic starlet. The perfect person to star in a cheesy fictional late 1980's early 1990s teen sitcom. Her life story would be somewhat similar to the 1950's starlet; she'd be an actress whose career would come to a mysterious and tragic end in her mid thirties.

Marilyn Monroe often worked in comedies with Director Billy Wilder, one of my favorite directors. One of his greatest films was the classic drama Sunset Boulevard. While Ms. Monroe wasn't in that film, it gave me ideas for Nikki Desmond, Marilyn's TV alter ego. It also gave me ideas for the plot of this story. Sunset Boulevard is the tragic story of faded 1920's silent film star Norma Desmond, a woman so obsessed with her quest to make a return to

Behind The Scenes

the spotlight she commits murder to achieve it. I loved the themes in that movie because they're so relevant today. As an actress gets older, she has fewer opportunities to showcase her talent due to narrowing standards of beauty in the entertainment industry that have become more and more youth obsessed over the years. Nowadays when an actress turns thirty she's considered over-the-hill by most producers and casting directors. A sad shame.

But not in my story.

I don't see a mid-thirties woman as old. I feel at that age a young woman is just coming into a sense of mental and emotional maturity. It'd be a great time for Marilyn's big break: A break away from Hollywood. Moving away to New York would allow her an opportunity to become a new character: Herself. It'd be an identity where she'd define herself on her own terms. She'd get a chance to actualize her potential working at a college. In that environment she'd come into a new way of thinking, one that contrasted the businesslike approach to the art we call entertainment in Hollywood. This happy ending would be the beginning of Marilyn's new story.

A deeper story was coming into focus than the original one I planned. It had more layers and substance than the original novel I was going to write. However, when I put my fingers to the keyboard to write the book it just didn't work as a novel. It seemed a story about Hollywood needed to be told in a Hollywood format: The screenplay.

I wasn't a stranger to screenwriting; on the suggestion of my sister I started studying the craft to build up my writing skills. I'd written a few adaptations of my novels *Isis* and *The Cassandra Cookbook* for practice, but never wrote a complete screenplay from scratch. The ideas for this story were so good I decided to go for it; after all it would be a great learning experience.

Inspired by Sunset Boulevard, Marilyn Monroe, and the 1990's teen sitcoms I used to watch I put my fingers to the keyboard and got to writing. I completed the first draft in a couple of months and was on my way through revisions on the second when tragedy struck:

My six-year-old laptop died.

It was the best thing that ever happened to me.

I was so obsessed with following rules regarding screenplay formatting and industry standards on page counts that I wasn't telling Marilyn's story. I was telling a Hollywood story. The original script was incomplete; some characters like Lucia, Shayla and Adam the Clown were horribly underdeveloped. Doing revisions by hand I rewrote Marilyn's story to my standards not Hollywood's. Marilyn's story was about walking away from traditional methods and doing things on one's own terms; I needed to practice what I preached. The story took a life of its own and the characters told their stories through me and it became Shawn James' story, not a Hollywood story.

I had a blast writing this book. I hope you enjoyed it.

Also Available From Shawn James

ISBN 978-1-60264-229-4.
Suggested Retail Price $14.95

A pinch of hard work.
A dash of determination.
A recipe for success.

Cassandra Lee's lifelong dream is to take over the Downtown Brooklyn bakery with her name on it when her parents retired. Her dream turns into a nightmare near the eve of her wedding when she learns corporate giant ITC Foods has plans for the store and her low down down low fiancé Gerald is caught in the arms of another man.

Cassandra perseveres, acting as her parents' agent working with ITC rep Simon James to complete the deal. As their professional relationship gets personal, Simon reveals a secret that devastates Cassandra. Sending Cassandra over the edge, Simon must come up with a plan to heal her broken heart and make her dreams come true.

Also Available From Shawn James

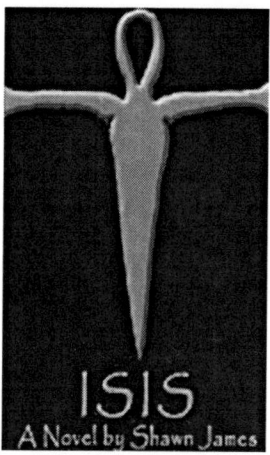

ISBN 1–58939–236–1
Suggested Retail Price $12.95

**A lost goddess
A heritage found.
A greater destiny to be achieved.**

In the aftermath of a horrible tragedy, Isis the long–lost daughter of Osiris has committed a heinous crime. Because she didn't receive guidance from her father, the elder gods show mercy on the young goddess by stripping her of her powers and imprisoning her on an uncharted island in the South Pacific.

Osiris and Queen Isis reunite with his long–lost child to begin the difficult process of establishing a familial relationship. Hoping to guide Isis towards the greater destiny she's supposed to fulfill, her parents begin teaching her the ways of the gods. However, Seth's herald E'steem lurks in the shadows offering Isis freedom for a price. Caught in the middle of a never–ending war between the gods, Isis must choose to either return to the troubled world she knows all too well, or take a journey down an unknown path where faith is her only guide.

Order Form

Did you enjoy this book? Want to buy it for a friend or as a gift? If you can't find it in stores, additional copies of this title are available directly from Shawn James. He'll even autograph them for you on request. Send a copy of this form **(DON'T CUT UP YOUR BOOK!)** and a **U.S. postal money order (NO CHECKS PLEASE!)** payable to:

SHAWN JAMES
1294 Grant Avenue #5A
Bronx, NY 10456–1320

TITLE	QTY	PRICE
ALL ABOUT MARILYN	_____	$14.00
THE CASSANDRA COOKBOOK	_____	$15.00
ISIS	_____	$13.00
Autograph	_____	FREE
Shipping charge		$ 7.00
(**NY** RESIDENTS ADD 8.375 sales tax per book)		$_____
TOTAL		$_____

NAME_____

ADDRESS_____

CITY_____**STATE**_____**ZIP**_____

Allow 3–5 weeks for delivery. US orders only. All sales final.